ORIGINAL "DR. PHIBES RISES AGAIN!" BOOK I I MOVIE TIE-IN FRONT COVER
PUBLISHED BY AWARD BOOKS 1972

IF DR. PHIBES TURNED YOUR BLOOD TO ICE, YOU WON'T WANT TO MISS THE TERRIFYING SEQUEL—
DR. PHIBES RISES AGAIN!

"Dr. Phibes, that bizarre evil genius, is back with all his old diabolic deviltry." —
Variety

Here is just one of the ways Phibes disposes of his enemies in this spellbinding book:

Shavers fled for his life through the corridors from which he had come. The eagle followed unerringly — swooping, screeching, extending its greedy talons.

Shavers knew he was doomed. The great bird swooped, missed, then dived again. This time the talons gripped the cloth, then flesh and bone, crushing the bone.

The bloody talons now held human flesh. The eagle fed ravenously . . .

Dr. Phibes Rises Again!

IT WILL KEEP YOU SHUDDERING TO THE LAST PAGE!

*You won't want to miss the first book
About the abominable DR. PHIBES.
Ask your local bookstore or order direct*

AS0869   **DR. PHIBES, by William Goldstein**

WILLIAM GOLDSTEIN

dr. phibes rises again!

BOOK II
of
THE CULT-CLASSIC
DR. PHIBES SERIES

ALSO BY
WILLIAM GOLDSTEIN

THE CULT-CLASSIC *DR. PHIBES* SERIES

Dr. Phibes

Dr. Phibes Rises Again!

Dr. Phibes In The Beginning

Dr. Phibes Vulnavia's Secret

dr. phibes rises again!

BOOK II
of
THE CULT-CLASSIC
DR. PHIBES SERIES

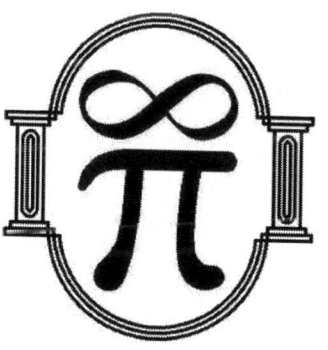

WILLIAM GOLDSTEIN

The characters and events in this book are fictitious. Any similarity to real persons, living or dead is coincidental and not intended by the author.

Copyright © 2014 by William Goldstein
All rights reserved. Except as permitted under the U.S. Copyright Act of 1976, no part of this manuscript may be reproduced, distributed, transmitted in any form or by any means, or stored in a database or retrieval system, without the prior written permission of the author.

Book design by Damon J.A. Goldstein
Copyright © 2013 by Damon J.A. Goldstein
Forever Phibes Icon and book plate design by
Damon J.A. Goldstein
Copyright © 2011 by Damon J.A. Goldstein

Published by Phibes Phorever Publishing

First Phibes Phorever Printing, October 2014
10   9   8   7   6   5   4   3   2   1

ISBN-13: 978-1502848420

Book design by Damon J.A. Goldstein
Cover design by Damon J.A. Goldstein
Art direction by Damon J.A. Goldstein
Phibes Forever Icon and book plate design by
Damon J.A Goldstein

ORIGINALLY PUBLISHED BY AWARD BOOKS 1971
Copyright © 1972 by
American International Productions (Eng.) Limited

Printed in the United States of America

$$\pi^2 = \infty + \frac{\infty}{\pi} = \frac{\infty}{\pi}$$

Formulaic Hypotitheñai
From The Dr. Anton Phibes Manifestos
- circa 1929

dr. phibes rises again!

by

WILLIAM GOLDSTEIN

Based on the screenplay by
James Whiton and William Goldstein

"Ere the ancient bone to ancient skeletons lie, Our fates can catch and scratch the sky. . . ." Ninth Canto "ELEGY OF ELEMENT"

Anton Phibes

dr. phibes rises again!

Chapter 1

It was hot. Awfully hot. The Sun Disk tested the air as it had for the last two hundred days. Certainly the sky must crack.

The streets caught the heat and multiplied it between baked walls. Sand drifts, sent in by an occasional desert wind, had long since added their sheen to the dusty walkways. What little commerce remained ground the sand further into the dust, so that the streets themselves glistened like the walls of a brick oven. It was a deceptive warmth, for at night the air hung low and cold in this bend of the river. And the townspeople—artisans, traders, and farmers — shivered anxiously now in the autumn of one more drought. Across the river the limestone cliffs caught their cries and made them into echoes. Tomorrow there would be fewer to wail.

But drought was among the least of Amarna's problems in that difficult year. The city, which had risen a half-century earlier to challenge, then surpass, the splendor of Thebes, now also knew starvation, isolation, and the darker fruits of decay. Bakers brought out their loaves but once a week, vendors piled their fruits atop pebbles to conceal the meagerness of the harvest, and the farmers, despairing of ever seeing the rain again, surrendered more and more of their homesteads to dust, finally fleeing singly, then in tattered groups, to the once great city. There they joined thousands of other survivors of that dust-swept season to seek alms in the limestone and diorite temples of Aton. This mass of outcast faithful could hardly have surmised that alms would not be forthcoming. And even if they had, their hunger and zeal would have blinded them to the Sun God's disfavor.

The few priests who remained thought different. Their revenues had long since been cut off by the Imperial Court. What little they collected toward the maintenance of the ornate complex of temples, shrines, and funerary edifices came from local citizens. It was not enough. For them, a remnant of the dedicated, who, either because of age or convictions, had elected to continue their service to the Aton, it was continually painful to watch the daily decay of his sacred establishment. They talked about it as they passed along the corridors, their voices subdued under the weight of stone, and remembered a better time, when faith was strong and its rewards most provident.

The very oldest remembered the beginning. Even before it was settled, Amarna beckoned to the traveler, situated, as it was, almost at the center point of the empire. Three hundred miles north from Thebes as the Nile flowed, the limestone cliffs flanking the river's east bank edged backward in a stately semi-circle, enclosing a lush amphitheatre of rich bottom land that offered infinite possibility, infinite reward. The site drew favorable comment from the warrior king Thutmose IV, but he was too busy with campaigns in Asia to encourage much development. It fell to his grandson, Amenhotep IV, to furnish Amarna with a grandeur commensurate with its setting.

This young man was an enigma even before he assumed the throne. He was tall, with elongated—even languid— features, and ungainly hands. Unlike his father and grandfather, he enjoyed neither the hunt nor the other martial arts that were supposed to be the mark of any young prince and, although the Egyptian land army was the best the world had seen up to that date, he made little use of that exceptional instrument. Amenhotep was not interested in conquest.

The prince fit well into court life. His dealings with the multitudes of functionaries were correct enough to keep palace affairs moving with unusual efficiency. The obligatory statutes to Amon were completed with equal dispatch. Couriers from Kush, Nubia, Canaan, and the lands beyond the Euphrates who came to Thebes in great numbers during those years were greeted by the future king with the proper mix of fact and diplomacy that makes for favorable foreign relations. But it was in the spiritual pursuits that the royal heir showed his earliest prowess.

His father, Amenhotep III, was a vigorous ruler who, with his wife, Tiy, built extensively in Egypt, Nubia, and the Sudan. He graced the capital with an enormous palace to serve as a showcase for his familial embellishments. He further startled the citizens by causing a large pleasure lake over a mile in circumference to be built close by. And, by way of public honor to his wife, he had an opulent barge built for the great lady so that the royal couple could enjoy the lake together in full view of the Theban populace. The king was no mere show-off, however. Other pharaohs before him revered the spiritual precepts that formed the backbone of the ancient culture. But Amenhotep III placed special emphasis on *Ma'at*, or "truth," taking for two of his names *Nab-Ma'at Re* ("The Lord of Truth is Re") and *Kha-em-Ma'at* ("He who makes appearance in truth"). To show the sincerity of his affection for *Ma'at*, the king conducted the exemplary affairs of his court life in full view of courtiers and visitors alike. In sum, the old king was a straightforward man; in the farthest reaches of his own simple faith he could not have been prepared for the extravagant and finally explosive wanderings of his son.

But he did appoint the young prince co-regent. Amenhotep IV assumed the throne and a portion of its burdens soon after he married Nefertiti, his piquant and equally powerful sister. Once enthroned, the new king demonstrated the courtly skills he had practiced as a prince, and was able to counter the inertia of the civil servants and the avarice of the priests because of his experience. The young couple further added to their popularity by living even more openly than their parents and, in fact, were subjects of much gossip, since the king was in the habit of hugging and fondling his queen in the presence of courtiers.

It was in the sixth year of his reign that Amenhotep IV first showed the independence of thought that later marked him as a seer, and still later as a heretic. He declared a jubilee celebrating not Amon, the local deity who was preeminent among all the gods, but rather Aton, the naked disk of the sun itself, an element previously obscure in the Egyptian spiritual outlook. He further astonished Thebes by declaring that he and his god had been ruling for the same length of time. The populace loved the festivities, while the priesthood grumbled. These minions, steeped in the severe orthodoxy of Amon, whose name had been ascendant above all other gods since the Twelfth Dynasty, looked with something less than favor upon such public adulation for a deity not of their own temple. Its implications in loss of power and prestige were not in the least attractive.

The grumbling mounted with each of Amenhotep's new pronouncements. The priests at Thebes sought and soon received commiseration from their brothers at Karnak. "Who was this upstart," they asked, "who shared his faith with an obscenity?" An attempt was made to speak to the young man through his wife, but Nefertiti was as resolute as her sire. She invited the delegation of elders to leave her chamber without offering them the customary bowl of fruits.

They next approached the guardian of the royal household and this man, whose courtly mien belied a penchant for secured opulence, lent the petitioners a much more willing ear. At their second meeting, to which he had brought some more officials of the royal household as well as the general director for building, Assamemnes (for that was that worthy's name), he spoke openly of his displeasure with the king and his ways. To the priests this stream of invective was as welcome as a miracle spontaneously produced from a shrine, and if a conspiracy wasn't hatched on the spot, these men, each a loyal public servant, at least had the makings of one in their grasp.

Their discussion turned to dismay when Amenhotep caused to be published, as part of the sacred literature of the state, the "Hymn to Aton." Its first two lines were particularly painful: "When thou settlest in the Western horizon/The land is in darkness like death." The hymn went on to extoll the singularity and strength of the Sun Disk, leaving quite literally no room in heaven or earth for Amon, Osiris, Re, or any of the other multitudinous deities whose temples flourished across the land. With one full-throated sweep, Aton's hymn cast them out, replacing their ancient and privileged dogmas with a new teaching that spoke of truth, of the unity of men, of the power and accessibility of the king.

Aton's hymn was immediately successful. The king's popularity rose; the clergy seethed. They were soon joined by the more powerful civil servants of Assamemnes' rank who had begun to have misgivings about a king who emphasized—it seemed at every turn—that *he* was the source of all truth. The spare, gawky youth had grown into a ruler whose awkward and ugly physique could be countenanced on the royal throne. They could not, however, forgive Amenhotep's rough handling of the power prerogatives once exclusively theirs. By way of retaliation the priests of Osiris' temple at Karnak consecrated a hymn to their own favorite deity. The verse ran to one hundred stanzas, with emendations. The massive work recorded the passage of most of Egypt's famous and lesser lights. It detailed their achievements and, in somewhat more obscure terms, their efforts beyond the pale. Appropriately the hymn's subtheme was moral, affirming Osiris' hand in all of this subject's progress.

News of the work was received with proper solemnity by Amon's acolytes. The temple, which had grown into a hotbed of intrigue, even provided couriers to assist with its publicizing. In the meantime the Osiris brotherhood busied itself with recording their accomplishment on papyrus. The resultant scroll occupied almost the entire volume of one of the temple's larger workrooms and required a team of twenty men to transport it to the shrine on the floor above for consecration. Even in this home of Osiris the ceremony was notably turgid, and as soon as the chief priest's last fetid words passed from his lips, the twenty bearers struggled anew to their task, sweating and groaning down the long corridors until they finally managed to restore the monstrous papyrus to the room of its birth. There it stayed like a fecund immortal onion, its strophes compressing each other in the darkness and, although the "Hymn of Osiris" was often quoted (and often misquoted), the priests who had generated that elephantine paean steadfastly refused to let it venture forth from its musty hiding place.

While the priests were going through their clerical ablutions, Assamemnes was pursuing other avenues toward the same objective: namely clipping the young Pharaoh's wings. His movements, as befitted a man of such girth, were ponderous, but his results came within a hair of being infinitely more successful.

In his official capacity as Director of Building, Assamemnes was obliged to spend a great deal of time travelling to the many sites—Karnak and Abydos were favorites—where the royal household was creating monuments to the national grandeur. It had become his habit to visit only the major works, leaving the smaller shrines to his many assistants. Assamemnes was a notorious carouser and womanizer and found life at court, with the excitement of Thebes close at hand, much more to his taste. However, as his disgruntlement grew, it occurred to his wine-bent mind that great profit might be derived if he were to gain the confidences of the many couriers whose business it was to maintain the flow of information to and from the capital.

He expanded his itineraries in detail, temporarily relinquishing the company of several ladies of the harem for what he correctly judged to be a more provident course. This burden of celibacy was a heavy one for the General Director, and many an evening found him groping to the wineshop in some dusty backwater town. There he would drink, fighting at once to wash the dust of his travels from his parched throat and to retain the name of the petty functionary he was courting for the moment. Often the wine would win, reducing the wheezing Assamemnes to a sleeping giant, his bulk cast across the table to the embarrassment of the rustics who, out of deference to his station, were afraid to disturb their important guest. At other times he was able to hang on to the thread of liquid conversation long enough to gain the halting confidence of his drinking companion. Invariably these messengers were honored, if not a bit startled, by the attention of so important a man. But the bonds of civil service are strong and durable, and most of his cronies proved quite willing to talk about their duties, seeing some possible reward or commendation for their work developing from their newfound contact.

Assamemnes was a master of survival in a world of public administration that was capable of reducing a less watchful man to a cipher. He played to their vanity, spoke affably, if a bit blandly, and revealed everything but his purpose in the process.

His rewards were quick in coming. Soon many of the couriers whom he had so assiduously courted made a point of visiting his offices in the palace whenever they were in town. On his home ground Assamemnes took pains to be discreet: he couldn't risk being accused of insubordination. He met his visitors in his formal offices in audiences attended by the appropriate number of secretaries. If Assamemnes was excited by these interludes he never showed it. His speech, rapid and circular in the extreme, was as far removed from the eager probing of gossip as possible. But the Director General of Buildings did glean a number of tempting bits of information about his master, all of which he judiciously filed away for future use. Among these confidences was the news, related by its bearer in the most animated terms, of a new installation at Amarna. The object in question was a *stela*, and the courier spent the best part of an hour describing its design in detail.

So moved was Assamemnes by this disclosure that he resolved to confide his information to the priests at the Temple of Amon that the *stela* was to be dedicated to their archrival. He waited for the appropriate time. But, as it turned out later, the General Director was, in his ponderous fashion, too late by a day to affect the momentous events which followed.

It was at that time that the king, who was then in his twelfth year of reign, announced that he was changing his, regal name to Akhenaton, to reflect the true faith of his office, and to further honor the prominence of this new faith in the land, he proclaimed that the capital of Egypt would henceforth be positioned at Amarna.

The move to Amarna was quiet; it was also emphatic. The strange, gawky youth, who had cut his teeth on palace intrigues, now showed that he had learned well the uses of men and power. With great finesse Akhenaton bound the junior civil servants to his cause by promising them wealth and position in the new government. His conquest of the priests was equally decisive. News of the Amarna shrines had throttled Thebes for months. Akhenaton merely let the gossip run its course, allowing it to become known that men of high faith and moral precepts were needed to guide Amarna's spiritual growth. Several hundred priests and neophytes were in Akhenaton's train in the first great move northward.

Also in that train were young nobles who had become excited at the prospects of new glories. Money, power, prestige—all seemed to glitter with the mention of Amarna. These men had shown drive and ability at Thebes, but the rigid traditions of their class placed a solid, stolid bulk of landed princelings between them and any opportunity of reward. These *parvenus* were ready to take as much as they could get.

Throughout the final preparations the grumbling, the jockeying for position, the confidences and the betrayals kept the comings and goings at the palace at a fever pitch. Those who had decided early to make the move tried to improve their position. Those who were sitting on the fence alternatively listened to the ones staying behind or worried if they were to be invited at all. The older potentates, like Assamemnes, fumed and plotted, but they could do nothing to stop the royal decision. Some enterprising vendors were even selling travel kits, complete with maps of building sites of the new city.

Akhenaton was greatly excited by these preparations and ordered his secretaries to help wherever they could. The complexity of the move's logistics soon became sufficiently apparent so that a coordinating office was set up to handle the mountain of details requisite to packing, grouping and transporting an army composed of some twenty thousand persons. The king's last official act before faking leave of the old palace was to order the erection of a colossal stone portrait of the royal couple. Significantly Akhenaton chose Karnak, the traditional site for such commemoration. Even more significantly, the king ordered that the bust of the queen should be the same size as his own. Previously the Pharaohs had portrayed their wives on a much smaller scale, placing them at their feet or standing in the background. It was Akhenaton's way of honoring Nefertiti for her dedication.

The regal train's entry into Amarna was a triumph. To greet and commemorate the event a grouping of fourteen tall *stelae* awaited the great host at the city's principal approach. Both in their language and their craft the tall columns were even more magnificent than the description that had charged Assamemnes' imagination. To insure good luck for their cause, Akhenaton had himself and his wife carried into Amarna atop a marvelously jeweled platform drawn by a team of trained horses. As they passed before the *stelae* at the gate to the new capital the marchers, who had all donned their most comely finery, roared approval of the royal couple so that it would later be recorded that all Amarna cheered when Akhenaton entered. The king had little doubt that it was a good omen for all time to come.

For the next two decades that spirit of adventure for high stakes carried the settlers and latecomers alike to a dazzling list of achievements in their new home.

The royal palace and its attendant government offices were completed in record time. A series of public buildings, each freshly designed in keeping with the new spirit of freedom, arose almost overnight, and the ring of homesteads circling the new capital expanded daily.
Everywhere arose the temples, shrines, and monuments in honor of the Sun Disk and Akhenaton rode everywhere to dedicate and consecrate his patron god.

During the feverish building, Akhenaton took special pains to secure his power throughout the land. To assure that the break with the past was complete, he sent out emissaries charged with the task of removing Amon's name from the public view. They hacked his likeness from granite monuments, tore it out of sacred papyri and even attacked the god in his own temples. His priestly servants, worn down from the effects of royal hostility, offered little resistance and kept their muttered curses to themselves, out of fear of more persecution. Akhenaton was less severe on the other chief gods, preferring officially to ignore Osiris while Re, whose main temple lay at Heliopolis, was brought in piecemeal to the prescribed devotions.

In his pursuit of *Ma'at*, the king triggered a wave of naturalism in the arts. Flowers, birds and people were all painted or carved in true likenesses down to the smallest warts and calluses. A painted bust of Nefertiti caught the hardened beauty of the great queen but didn't fail to register her rather long neck in the process. The conservative painters, poets and writers witnessed the flow of art objects from Amarna with shock and an increasingly acid commentary.

These criticisms—and they were always in a small voice—didn't disturb the royal composure which, if anything, was demonstrating an even firmer rule.

Excited by the pace of development and enraptured by the natural beauty of Amarna, Akhenaton was engulfed by his zeal toward the Sun Disk. In the new capital, across the land, and in the provinces as far away as Sasebi, near the third Nile cataract, construction extolling the Aton sprang up in a torrent of religious feeling. Within a few years Akhenaton was so secure that he declared himself to be the son of the Aton. Thereafter, Egyptians worshipped the king and the king worshipped his god.

For a few years Akhenaton's star glowed brightly. His

name was praised across the land. Everywhere his words were treated like heavenly rite; his deeds were the subject of myth and riddle; and his family life, exposed in its finest detail, was emulated by the good citizens of Egypt. The army, whose generals had wisely sat out the early controversies, lent their stiffening to the Amarna government, no doubt supplying a necessary tot of courage to the officialdom in the face of its many detractors. For a brief moment Amarna, in fusing the many national gods into one, achieved a unity of spirit hitherto unknown in Egypt. The capital, sensing its own greatness, tottered at the edge of destiny and praised its king. It was Akhenaton who had moved the seat of government from Thebes. It was Akhenaton who had broken the old ruling order. It was Akhenaton whose zeal sustained the conscious excellence of Amarna—and it was Akhenaton who transfixed an article of faith into a driving spiritual concept. Amarna gathered its breath and praised their king aloud.

But it didn't, couldn't last. Bad times fell upon Amarna soon enough. The loss of revenues from the outlying provinces exacerbated the economy, which was already strained by the large numbers of persons displaced (and still disgruntled) by the government's move to Amarna. But neither the gradual collapse of the empire nor the growing dissent at home shook the king as much as the official visit paid him by his mother, Tiy.

The Dowager Queen still maintained residences in Thebes where she had repaired after her husband's death. Her relations with her son were correct and her visits to the dazzling Amarna court, although infrequent, were always cordial. Her trip to Akhenaton in his twelfth Amarna year was no exception; she toured the city with the royal couple and appeared relaxed—even serenely happy—at a variety of state functions. The first inkling that something had gone wrong was Nefertiti's exile from the palace a few months after Tiy's departure. Shortly after the king's favorite, Smenkh-ka-Re, was appointed co-regent. Within a year that worthy had returned to Thebes, the tandem government tottering for another few years before it fell in favor of Nefertiti's half-brother, Tut-Ankh-Amon.

Amarna ceased to be the power when the new king re-established his government at Thebes. The city that had known glory in one dazzling instant saw its fate sealed when the new king took, as his official name, Tut-Ankh-Amon, but by that time many had fled the erstwhile capital. To *those* who stayed on remained only their broken dreams.

Pi Ankhi was one of these. He had been chief servitor to Akhenaton and felt honor-bound to preserve the memory of his king. During its decline he had served as a rallying point for the steadily declining band of the faithful who had remained at Amarna. They met in small groups to talk longingly about past glory and how they might change the harsh realities of their life. In this there was little hope, for the Theban government, first under Tut-Ankh-Amon and now led by the general, Har-em-hab, had grown increasingly vigorous in its efforts to obliterate the heresies of the Aton. As he had done to Amon, Akhenaton's name was gouged from all of his memorials. Trade with Amarna was heavily taxed and travel to and from the city was proscribed. Under these conditions the city barely supported itself; the drought it was now enduring was rapidly reducing Amarna to a desert.

Pi Ankhi reflected on these sober circumstances as he made his way along the dust-covered streets. His once strong frame was bent now against the relentless wind. It brought a taste of salt to his mouth, a bad sign. The government's agents must have wasted a few more fields. His legs hurt. The walk was making him tired. He smiled a little at the thought that in old age, one doesn't require as much food. He didn't think of himself as old, but as a practical man the chief servitor knew that one must make certain decisions.

Pi Ankhi had lived a busy if unspectacular life. His job had been to look after the king's personal effects and to provide them for his use when called upon. He was excellent at schedules, classification, and making do with the materials at hand. He was known to his colleagues at the court as a man whose word was good. He was among the first to come to Amarna and steadfastly believed in the city's dream long after its brilliant but brief example crumbled. Akhenaton prized above all others the quality of loyalty in men; his last assignment to Pi Ankhi was a fitting royal acknowledgment.

The Chief Servitor quickened his pace as he thought of the king's final instructions: "No one living now must see my grave," Akhenaton had said. "Perhaps in ten generations hence they will comprehend our faith. It will be soon enough then for them to gauge its truth."

Akhenaton then entrusted the architect's plans for the royal burial chamber to him. The king had chosen the site well. The tomb would be dug in the mountain that commanded the hills on the opposite bank of the Nile. Its entrance would be through a series of tunnels, with the main exterior gate situated on the reverse side of the mountain so that one would have to approach it from the desert. Akhenaton had given Pi Ankhi further orders to visit Karnak to check on the cutting of certain stone blocks there. Then the two men shook hands and parted. It was the last time that the Chief Servitor would see his king alive.

He bent closer to the dun walls of the buildings to get out of the main force of the winds. He would have to be careful in crossing the river. He didn't want to be followed. He knew most of the people in Amarna by sight, but strangers frightened him; they might be agents. At that thought he fingered the gold key in his pocket. His fingers trembled a bit.

He crossed the last major square before the waterfront docks and could now see the Nile in the middle distance. He was happy to see that the sun was hanging just above the horizon. He would be across the river at dusk, lessening his chances of being tracked. He would return after dark, but that was no matter.

He had just started to cross the square when he spotted three men standing near a deserted fountain at its center, none of whom he recognized. He couldn't take the risk of passing too close, so he slowly altered his course. Forty . . . thirty . . . twenty paces to go. They hadn't looked at him. He closed and was even with them, his legs straining now to carry him past the point where they might look directly in his face. Finally he made it, breathing faster but still walking sharply. His momentum carried him to the docks where he quickly hailed a boat, jumping into it and ordering the oarsman away. He fixed his eye on the opposite bank. Only after they were well out into the river did he chance a backward look. The square was empty.

The air was violet with the coming night as Pi Ankhi picked his way along the rock defiles to the tomb's single entrance on the river side, well-concealed by boulders. This passageway, as well as the main one on the opposite side of the mountain, were to be flooded, thus creating a twin subterranean river in the center of which rose the main burial chamber containing Akhenaton's remains, protected by water all around and the mountain above. The flooding was controlled by a series of valves hewn in the rock. The doors to the central vault would be sealed and made watertight by locking them with the eagle-shaped key Pi Ankhi now held in his pocket. The king's instructions on these matters were quite explicit; they were less explicit on when to put the plan into operation. Akhenaton had said merely that he wanted no person living then to view his remains. With government becoming ever more bold in its obliteration of Akhenaton's memory, Pi Ankhi judged that it was only a matter of time before the order was given for the removal of his master's sarcophagus to Thebes where, he knew, it certainly would be destroyed. As usual, the Chief Servitor's timing was precise.

Very quickly Pi Ankhi located the small opening and ducked inside. The trip across the river had refreshed him, and his movements were now all proper, direct, and with no wasted motion. He lit a candle and quickly located the first valve a few paces down from the passageway. He slid the rounded stone lever forward and heard the rush of water through the rock channels. It had gone well so far. He trotted up the graded tunnel, gaining the entrance to the main burial chamber just as the water began to seep along the tunnel floor.

Pi Ankhi was surprised at the sparse furnishings of his master's tomb. The large outer room contained only two items. The first was a small shrine to Aton with the legend, "I will light my son's passage on the river of life" inscribed on its base. The second object was a long, slender barge carved from a single ebony log. Pi Ankhi paused long enough to inspect the barge's equipment. Sail, rudder, maps and stores all seemed in order. Then he noticed a small chest that bore his name. Startled, he picked it up and opened it.

Inside were two vials with a small scroll, bearing the official seal, instructing him to remove the box and its contents to his own burial vault so that when the appropriate time came he could make the journey on the River of Life with his Pharaoh.

He was still shaking slightly as he entered the second, smaller room that contained Akhenaton's sarcophagus. Holding the candle a bit higher he murmured a brief prayer for their friendship, then slipped out. Somehow he felt the need to hurry.

He locked the outer door to the burial chamber according to his instructions. Then, pocketing the eagle-shaped key and the box, he negotiated the long downward ramp that led ultimately to the main exit and entrance. This was protected by a maze closer to the opening, but here the ramp ran down, then up, being intersected at its low point by another set of ramps that led to the workmen's rooms elsewhere in the mountain. When he reached the intersection Pi Ankhi activated the second valve that would flood the ramps and mazework up to the cave at the main entrance. That completed his work and he hurried up the incline, anxious to be on his way home before the night's dampness could start his bones aching again.

Now he groped his way along the caves' interiors and could smell the outside air, cooler and damper than the constricted atmosphere inside the mountain. Pleased with his night's work, he began to think how well he had served his Pharaoh.

At that something hard, raw and urgent burst directly behind his eardrum. He collapsed on the floor of the cave, the blood boiling out of a jagged tear in his head. He was unable to complete his thought before he died, and had no way at all of preventing the man—who was at that moment bending over his body—from taking the eagle key and the box containing the means of his final transport from his pocket.

Chapter 2

"Jonathan, I don't propose to tell you your business. God knows what it is you've got up your sleeve this time, but four hundred thousand pounds is high stakes in anybody's game— especially when you're going into the desert with only Allenby's military charts to go on. They were dated before Khartoum fell." Adam Ambrose snubbed his cigar into the thick glass ashtray. A whisk of ash overshot the edge, spraying across the top of his black tuxedo trousers. "Dammit, I'll burn these pants before I get to the dance. Usually takes me three or four doubles before I'm into these tricks."

"Here's your first of the evening, Adam, to help celebrate the christening. Those are new trousers, aren't they?" Biderbeck lifted a tall whiskey and soda to his friend who was already slapping at the particles of ash in his lap. With all his bulk Adam Ambrose was a confirmed bungler. For the obese, a twist of the finger or a tweak of the nose often covers such awkwardness. But the Professor wasn't obese; he was portly, and the bulbousness of his extremities made him seem even more ponderous. By now his hands were making huge slapping sounds against his thighs. With each slam his feet kicked up like two great leather paddles.

"Of course they're new," he grumbled through wheezes, "I burned my last pair at the York baccalaureate. Had me up for some honorary degree. By the time I got off the podium the locals were through the canapés and punch. Didn't get a drink 'til I got back to London that midnight!"

Biderbeck had to muffle a laugh while he stirred his own drink. Even so, the heavy man heard him. "It wasn't so funny at the time, especially on the train coming back. Middle of June and the train was packed with people going out on holiday. Hot as a bath house there in the car, and me with my coat on."

"The ways to knowledge aren't always smooth, are they, Adam?"

"Now you are a fine one to talk, Jonathan. You've been gadding about for the past two decades all over the Near and Middle East, up into Hungary and the Scandinavias. Last month it was Skellig Michael."

The heavy man glanced down at his pants, saw that the streaks of ash still lined his paunch, and began pawing and brushing its considerable expanse with his free hand. But this was clammy from the drink, with the result that Professor Ambrose, as he did in so many other minor tasks, managed to give his trousers a thoroughly ruined look. Wheezing and clucking he worked his jowls into a sweated rage before giving it all up.

"Let me call Bruno and have them pressed, Adam," Biderbeck offered.

"Don't be silly. It'll take him an hour to get around these slacks. Besides, I rather like that old saw about the baggy-trousered professor... *esprit* and all that. But tell me—what keeps your spirit up, Jonathan? You've been the subject of at least one hundred technical papers... guest lecturer at the cream of the universities... written, discussed and argued over in the Sunday supplements. You've even brought a comparable fame—or should I say notoriety— to that Caenarvon chap, although he should be given some kind of medal for his persistence." The heavy man paused to catch a breath, blinking at his host in almost pained concern.

Biderbeck motioned him into a chair where Ambrose, after seeking out its extreme dimension with his girth, inhaled a full half of his drink and continued.

"I don't know if it's age or my other 'accomplishments,' but your energies would exhaust a man half our years— and you're really not that much younger than me, my good man . . ." Ambrose's voice trailed off, but Biderbeck's attention had already drifted and he now sat staring at the long wall of his library. There was enough on those shelves to furnish the most thorough contemplations. Neatly stacked amongst the polished walnut bindings were books, not show books in tooled leathers but a scholar's workshop, heavy in the specialized literature of archaeology and exploration but also well-stocked with histories, contemporary affairs, and even a shelf of some nineteenth century French poets. Ranged before this edifice were showcases, pedestals, and low tables on which were displayed a curious and marvelous assortment of domestic articles, weapons and religious goods sufficient to the wealth of the room. Many of the items were Egyptian, with the most prominent being a small sarcophagus, no doubt belonging to a child. This exquisite work, lacquered sandalwood inlaid with gold leaf, would have been a featured display in any museum. That it was not was no small comment about Jonathan Biderbeck's dimension as a man.

In fact, there was little knowledge to be gained about Biderbeck other than what was evidenced in his collections. He was dark, and a full shock of black hair framed his face.

He was handsome, dominantly so, with polished skin over taut features, very black eyes and a small mouth that smiled little. He tended toward dark suits that were in fashion rather than fashionable. He was the kind of man one could find interesting at first glance and, after making his acquaintance, one could continue to be fascinated. He was a mystery without being mysterious, a friend of his friends and nothing more, correct in general affairs, taciturn, unshowy, bizarre. No one really knew Jonathan Biderbeck although many sought his acquaintance. His poise, his bearing, the heat of his eyes and the trend of his voice in even the gentlest of conversation held out the hope of arenas of knowledge, vast recollections of delight, and a prescience of all that one questioned, all that one yearned to perceive. In a word, Jonathan Biderbeck was as timeless as all the vast pyramids, temples and other funereal architecture of an Egypt that had been his obsession for the better part of a lifetime.

He was a different man at work. The reserve, the steel concentration were there, but fused into a direction that imposed itself on others. In the early years Biderbeck had attached himself to several of the University-and privately-sponsored expeditions that were then organizing archaeology into a science. He went as an amateur, designed his own equipment, and approached each project with a meticulous precision that often yielded results when others in his group failed. He was among the first to advocate the use of the grid pattern in excavation, a technique which later brought to view, intact, the splendor of Karnak.

But Jonathan Biderbeck soon tired of the pedantry of these organized tours and thrust out on his own. His expeditions were planned with the precision of a military operation, and because he traveled light and moved fast he ran over the competition. Needless to say his tactics didn't endear him to his colleagues, but Biderbeck cared little for popularity. He kept to himself, announced his plans to no one, and continued to prick the smugness of the professionals. His work at Luxor in 1921 put Biderbeck in the news. Thereafter, like it or not, he was a regular topic of conversation to an adventure-hungry public who followed the developments in Egypt much as sixteenth century man traced the explorations of the New World. Had he cared to, Biderbeck probably could have attracted a broad following, but the kind of loyalty he demanded precluded this: he insisted on seeing a project through no matter what the hazards or what the costs. Of these last there had been many. A truck packed with furnishings from the Valley of Kings was lost to a flash flood in 1925. An advance camp in the Western Desert was wiped out by a sandstorm in 1928, and a cave-in during his 1932 excavations in Luxor nearly took the life of two graduate students.

But if these setbacks discouraged Biderbeck he never showed it. Decades after he had begun, he was still the cool, calculating craftsman. If anything, his hand was steadier now, and his appearance, the black steel calm of his features, had not changed a bit.

Ambrose watched him finish his drink in silence. The fire in the grate on the wall opposite blazed at full clip, filling the room with sputtering fumes from the oak logs. Even in repose, Biderbeck's movements were a study in economy. At slow intervals he swept the tall glass to his lips, drinking silently. Otherwise, he was completely still. Five, ten minutes passed. Then he spoke again, as if he hadn't stopped.

"You think we won't find it but of course you're wrong, Adam. The theme is as old as Djoser and the Great Pyramid.

It weathered two major invasions—the Hyksos and the Sea Peoples—and was still the single unifying force for a culture that was already thirty centuries old when Mark Antony was being wooed and won by Cleopatra."

"I'm not clear about what you're saying, Jonathan, and from all your verbal gymnastics I'd conclude that you're not clear either." Ambrose spoke slowly, holding his head down. He was still trying to repair the damage in his lap.

"Ideas disgust me. There's nothing so deadly as last year's novel, unless it's some philosopher's notion of a 'first principle.' If you can't see it, touch it, measure it—then it doesn't exist." Biderbeck swept up Ambrose's glass and started to refill the ice cubes and Scotch. He moved so fast that the bulky man looked up from his trials.

"You mention a unifying force in one breath, and your disgust with ideas in the next— and four hundred thousand pounds is four hundred thousand pounds! Now, as leader of an expedition that will subject a party of six persons to the mixed joys and hazards of the desert for a long enough period of time to make them sick of the dust and flies, good sense requires one to ask you, Jonathan, just what is it you're after?"

While Ambrose was unburdening himself, his cheeks getting ruddier with each word, Biderbeck had come up with the drinks and now stood looking down at his discomfited partner over the iced glasses. His lips turned in an ever-so-slight smile.

"I can see you're going to need a little more information." Biderbeck's voice was a murmur.

"Your understatement, like your entire aspect, Jonathan, is charming. I love a mystery as much as anyone, but I think it should be pointed out that with less than ten days remaining, it might be helpful—even provident for the entire party, including yourself, Jonathan—if you were to give us some clear specifics as to the 'what' and 'why' of our trip." He took a sip, then, catching his second wind, bulled on. "I mean, it's all very well to say that we're going to have a grand 'adventure,' that we'll be 'tapping at the roots of our life,' or that our little group will be 'crossing a trail untracked for centuries,' and to use any other of the hundreds of nuances with which you've flowered our planning sessions—but we're rapidly coming past the point of all that." Ambrose' voice fell lower. "I think its time for you to show and tell, Jonathan."

Biderbeck tapped his glass, drank and moved, or rather stalked toward a wall paneling. His voice held at the same compressed equilibrium.

"Egyptian life is bound up with the flow of the Nile. Every explorer from Champollion and Maspero to Flinders Petri and Schliemann on down to the moderns have known it, have studied it, and have tried to gauge the impact of that river's cycles on the people that lived on its banks. What is it that makes the Nile different? There are other great rivers of the world, all of them supporting populations of one kind or another. But only the Nile, tracking two thousand miles from Lake Victoria to the delta, through an enormous wasteland of harsh inhospitable deserts, sparked a civilization that was to last fifty centuries and produce some of the most startling architectural achievements ever to grace those or any other surroundings. The Egyptians celebrated life and prepared for death. In the process they honored a variety of gods whose beneficence they sought in making the transition between the two states."

"Yes, yes, of course—Amon, Re, Thoth . . . all that funerary paraphernalia." Ambrose shook his glass impatiently.

"And many more; moving one's earthly joys to the nether world always presented a problem. And, because everyone from king to commoner had certain aspirations for the after-life, the various religious centers gathered large and dedicated followings. Re's people at Herakleiopolis attracted the pilgrims. The cult of Amon established Thebes as a national capital. Traditionally and in practice the emphasis was on death, and the burial ceremony and subsequent commemoration concentrated on its preparation and smooth translation. This 'funerary outlook,' as you put it, Adam, dominated Egyptian religious thought throughout history. But there was one brief period when an idea, caught and driven by the imagination of one man, took hold, flared an instant, shedding an explosion of cultural and political changes in its wake, only to fall back into the awesome silence of reaction: that idea was the restoration of life. And that man was . . ."

"Akhenaton!" Ambrose shot the name back at his host. "The Heretic King!"

Biderbeck stopped for a moment, then moved back from the wall. "A value judgment, Adam."

"Call it what you want. When Akhenaton, or Amenhotep IV, as he was called then, assumed the throne, Egypt's empire was at its peak. Twenty years later she had lost the Asian provinces and most of Nubia—and Akhenaton was in disgrace."

"He bit off more than he could chew. The cult of Amon was too well-entrenched, and the move to Amarna threw most of the civil service in with the priests."

"He was unfit to rule. There's no disgrace in being an incompetent—if you're able to gather around you people who can keep control. Akhenaton, despite his idiosyncrasies, still wanted to *rule*. His willfulness proved his, as well as his country's undoing." Ambrose looked sharply at Biderbeck. "So that's it. You're going to Amarna, aren't you, Jonathan? But why? Its a dustbowl. The sorry remnants of a foolish experiment! What can you possibly expect to find?!"

Biderbeck, who had been pacing back and forth, pulled up short and, glancing at the lumbering Ambrose, pressed a segment of the wood. It slid open, gliding on some internal gear mechanism, making not a sound. Ambrose's beefy face sagged, then dropped blank. Was there no end to this strange man's surprises? Biderbeck's hands kept moving with the same economy, the same surgical precision. They were inside the wall now. Ah, he had found it; he was bringing it out. Ambrose leaned forward in his chair, a painful exertion for a man of his bulk. He could feel his ears pinging. His breath came short. Had he had too much to drink?

"My God, Jonathan, is that what I think it is?" Ambrose's face was pale from his many interior strains.

"What *do* you think it is?"

The papyrus glowed in Biderbeck's hands, a luminous diffusion that didn't completely come from the quartz light bulb above. It was a beautifully-colored segment about two feet in length and eighteen inches wide, sealed in airtight plastic. The whole was surrounded by an exquisite gold frame. Ambrose squinted. "Why it's . . . unless it's a marvelous copy it's one of the fragments . . ."

Biderbeck held it close for the heavy man to see better. "It is *not* a copy . . . and it *is* the middle section of the Osiris papyrus of the Twentieth Dynasty. Its weighty predecessor is lost. Of this one, the right-hand segment, which fits here, is, of course, in the treasure room at St. Petersburg, forbidden to any scholar. The left-hand segment was reported to have been removed to the hands of a private collector, a mysterious gentleman no one could ever really trace..."

Ambrose had recovered and his face was ruddied up with more than his usual excitement. "But how did this fall into your hands? It must have cost a bloody fortune! It was supposed to have disappeared when Constantinople was sacked in 1520."

"Ah, it did. And there were other 'prices' one had to pay." Biderbeck looked at his colleague, who was now bent almost double along the edge of his chair. The doubt, the garrulousness had drained from the man's face and he was—astonishingly so for so fat a man—eager. He decided to set the bait. "But if my interpretation of these hieroglyphics is even ninety per cent accurate . . . you have my word that *you* can take credit..."

Ambrose's ears pricked. "Take credit for what? It's your show!"

"Take credit for anything you wish—and keep anything else we find."

Ambrose puzzled. "You mean you actually give credence to that River of Life business?..."

"Akhenaton was a responsible man. Like all practical revolutionaries he knew precisely what he wanted, precisely how he was going to go about getting it"

"But Jonathan, you're getting into the realm of myths and spells. The Egyptians were great ones for all that mumbo jumbo. Regardless of whatever else he was, Akhenaton didn't have it in him to pull off a miracle. Besides, the priests of Amon were quite efficient. They spent fifty years paying back their debt to Akhenaton. The only record we're likely to find," Ambrose nodded at the papyrus, "will be in the dust."

"As I said, Adam, the credit on this one is yours. We've

worked together for a long time and I intend to prove you wrong, so let's drink to our return at which time you will be rich, famous and respectable and my life's work will be over." Biderbeck raised his glass. The fat man lifted his slowly, a bit reluctantly. Before they could seal the toast the room's atmosphere, as often happens in the presence of a beautiful woman, changed perceptively. The lady's voice, high and hard, immediately got to the heart of things.

"No, Jonathan, only *tonight's* party will be over if you two don't hurry, and Princess Frederica will never again invite you, Professor Ambrose, or you, Jonathan Biderbeck." Her voice softened to a purr. "Or Jonathan Biderbeck's ward. And I assure you I'm very interested in seeing who's wearing what, and who's doing what."

The girl slid into Biderbeck's arms, dispelling the mystery from that dark man's being with a rush of kisses and other silken gestures that were either the outpourings of a young girl's love or a very artful facsimile.

Ambrose had never been sure about Diana Trowbridge but he liked her simply because she was so damned engaging—and he was too much of a man of honor to cater to the gossip that roiled up about his colleague when Diana's presence in Biderbeck's affairs first became known. Not that Biderbeck had lost his head and gone charging about like a middle-aged stag; the man's bearing was too well-tuned for that. But after all, he was twice her age. He had installed her in his residence, and he did insist on escorting her everywhere. It was only when Biderbeck began showing her off at parties that Ambrose was pushed to extend himself. The men, and particularly the husbands, adored Diana immediately. On top of the fact that she wore her cornsilk blonde hair long to accentuate her smashing figure, Diana fancied the exclusive creations of Mainbocher and Christian

Dior. This goaded the women, infuriating the wives past the point of all reasonable decorum. Some of the conversations that Ambrose was privy to were absolutely vicious. At Lady Bentinck's Derby reception, Diana was called a harlot in some of the drawing room chatter; the smashing leopard coat she'd chosen for the occasion didn't help matters. Ambrose spent the entire time protecting the morality of his colleague, a losing position for him under the circumstances. That day he became so frazzled he misplaced his tout sheet—the list of selections he'd spent six hours deducing the previous evening—and crowned the afternoon by getting shut out at the betting windows. But Biderbeck remained imperturbable through the entire first shock of his splash into society, and if he heard any of the running commentaries on himself and his personal habits, he never showed it. Gradually the novelty wore off. Diana was accepted into the couple's chosen circles precisely as Biderbeck had announced her, and he and his "ward" continued to receive many more invitations than they could handle.

"And I'm interested in dancing with you all night even if you are my guardian." She shifted, brushing Biderbeck's ear with a small bite. Biderbeck edged back into the chair from the silken onslaught.

"Obviously I brought the girl up badly. She's much too demanding." Biderbeck was fighting to retain his decorum. Ambrose thought the whole thing enormously amusing but he wouldn't have dared to show it. The dear girl brought out something close to happiness from the dark man's iron depths. Far be it from Ambrose who, as a confirmed bachelor, understood well enough the personal wastage from spending too many nights alone, to question whatever it was his partner had found.

"Diana, I think he brought you up perfectly . . . especially if you'll allow me to have one of those dances. Especially if it's a Charleston."

"Done!" Diana jumped out of her patron's lap and called out into the hallway. "Bruno!"

All business now, she whisked away the glasses and ashtrays and was helping Biderbeck out of his smoking jacket when the manservant entered. Bruno was a huge hulk of a man, and other than the fact that Biderbeck had brought him back from one of his Near East trips, nothing was known about him. Some said that he was descended from the toughest of all land fighters, the Turkish janissaries. Others called him a Levantine pirate. Most people who had seen Bruno handle the amenities for his employer during their public appearances imagined the man to be either a detective or a thug. In fact, the forceful uncertainty of his presence served to thicken the mystery about the man who employed him.

He held Biderbeck's brocade dinner jacket while Diana hurried her charges along. "Don't you two ever get tired talking Egypt, Egypt, Egypt, and tombs, tombs, tombs?"

She captured Ambrose and proceeded to brush his lapels. The man absolutely blushed. A weak "Speak for yourself, Jonathan," was about all he could muster.

Biderbeck ignored the patient Bruno while he replaced the papyrus and locked the panel shut. Then, as if to terminate the conversation, he moved to one of the display tables which contained a well-detailed topographical model of the Amarna area. "You have a way of asking the perfect question at the perfect time, Diana. Allow me one short minute to answer this one, and we'll be on our way."

"One minute and no more, darling. Remember Princess Frederica is waiting."

Biderbeck removed the top of one of the containers to reveal a scale drawing depicting an intimate series of chambers, passageways and entrances. "From "The instructions for King Merikare' we learn that 'A man remains over after death and his deeds are placed beside him in heaps. However, existence yonder is for eternity, and for him who reaches it without wrongdoing, he shall exist yonder like a God.' That's the essential principle of the Egyptian funerary religion and it served them throughout their long history. An Egyptian further believed that Osiris would pass final judgment upon him, balancing his heart against the 'Ma'At' or truth. Now, it's human nature to hope for the best and all Egyptians, pragmatic as they were, looked forward to passing this test and spending the rest of eternity enjoying the best of the life they'd known on earth. It follows that they paid as much attention as they could to their personal burial preparations. For the average Egyptian only the meanest of graves awaited due to the limitations of his pocketbook. Pharaoh, however, could engage in his plans for eternity on a grand scale. The pyramids came into vogue during the Old Kingdom; these were massive, expensive and, as it later proved, impractical structures in a very significant sense. The Middle Kingdom saw the return of Mastebas, which often were little more than burial vaults covered by rock slab. It was during the Empire that the rock burial vaults such as the one depicted here, came into use."

"Jonathan!"

"I know, I know, the dear princess will start hatching. But surely Her Expediency can grant us a few more seconds." Biderbeck quickly bent to the model where he removed one face to reveal a cross section, showing the slanted passageways and a series of chambers in detail. "The pyramids were impractical because they didn't keep out the graverobbers. And, because the Pharaohs wanted to enjoy a similarly high standard of living in the hereafter, they made a point of stocking their final resting places with the best of their possessions. Many of their tombs were vast apartments literally crammed with furniture, food, ships and chests of jewels. They were, in a word, excellent 'marks.' This is a model of a fortified vault, designed especially to prevent the robbers from having their day which, measured as the time Pharaoh hoped to enjoy his occupancy, was indeed a long one. Interior passages all have been plugged with stone blocks. The outer entrances are concealed by landslides. And the vault proper is surrounded by a subterranean river."

"Jonathan, from what you've shown us there's a good chance we'll reach Egypt and never get to what it is you're after, even if you've got the location plotted and all that."

Biderbeck smiled at the girl, who had squared off against him across the table. "Adam, the lady has made her point." He glanced at the fat man who was struggling into his coat, then turned to stare full into the gorgeous features of the girl's face. "Diana, eight weeks from now we three and all the others will be standing somewhere under those mountains. I promise you, Adam, you will have uncovered a tomb richer than that of Tut-Ankh-Amon's. You, my sweet, will have had an adventure like few others. And I will have found what I want." His voice began to fail, "And I'll never mention Egypt or its secrets again."

Ambrose finally outwrestled his coat and took the girl's arm.

"Now tell me, Diana, in case it *is* a Charleston . . . do I kick with my right when you kick with your left—or vice versa?"

Biderbeck retrieved his coat from Bruno and followed them out the door. "We'll be out until a bit after midnight.

Stay here in the library . . . and help yourself to the whiskey."

Bruno nodded and closed the door, double-locking it from the inside.

It was cold—colder than it should have been for that time of year.

Biderbeck slipped the white silk scarf from his pocket and knotted it about his throat against the chill. He was glad to see that Ambrose had started up the car.

Chapter 3

He was getting nervous and he didn't like it. Pretty soon his hands would start to sweat and his throat would dry out. He had wanted to go out earlier to run it off, but that bitch had made him take her to the dry cleaner. The stop wasn't that far away but he had to drive down some awfully narrow streets—really more like alleys—where you had to watch that the fenders didn't scrape against the buildings. The day he got the Duesenberg, Mr. Biderbeck told him that the car was in his trust and no one else was to handle it. He would have to keep it waxed and polished, check on the mechanic so that he wouldn't cheat them too badly, make sure that the map case had all the correct charts, order the licenses and insurance on time, and see to all the other hundreds of details that go into maintaining one's automobile. It was a big job, but Mr. Biderbeck trusted him to do it and that made him proud. Just the day before yesterday he had seen this special beeswax at the chemist's, hard yellow bricks wrapped in white paper. He asked Mr. Jenkins if the wax would take a good polish. The chemist allowed that it would, although the manufacturer was selling the beeswax for sealing envelopes and other such things at a price too high for everyday use. Bruno didn't have to hear any more; he had paid Jenkins five shillings out of his own pocket and rushed home with his discovery.

That afternoon he brought out the buckets, cheesecloth and chamois to get the car ready for its weekly washing. First he drove it around to the shady side of the garage, being careful to sweep the macadam clear of any leaves and dust. Then he took a whiskbroom to the leather cushions, working on the higher spaces with a set of camel hair brushes he had bought especially for the purpose. When the wood was shining and free of dust, he rolled up the windows and shut and locked the door. Then, slipping into his coveralls, he selected the oldest, supplest piece of chamois and started to rub the car's surfaces. He had learned from experience that road dust, once wet, was a lot harder to get off than if left dry. It formed into a streaky paste hard enough to scratch wax. He took special care with the chamois, rolling and kneading it to the hard metal and chrome until the surface was slick and smooth. Every once in awhile he stood back from the car to check his handiwork. Finally, when the doors, grille and the length of the S-shaped fender all gave off the same glow, he felt ready to begin the actual washing. But there was one more detail: the car's underside. Glad at having remembered this crucial step, Bruno went into the garage to fetch the sliding mechanic's dolly he used to work under the car. He had to grope about in the heavy dust that smelled of leather and motor oil, finally stumbling across the dolly against some copper tubing where he had stacked it a week earlier. When he slid under the car he was glad he had taken the trouble, because the whole undercoating was covered with Midland mud from their trip the past Thursday. He really put the wire brush to it, and it required a half-hour of steady rubbing and clawing before Bruno felt he was ready to get on with the washing.

For this part of it he followed a very special formula. First he hosed the car down with cold water. Then he made a bucket of hot suds using the castile soap he kept in the linen closet. This he sloshed on the car with the cheesecloth, scrubbing down with the bristle brush. When the car was thoroughly lathered, he hosed it clean. Then, without letting the surface drain, he splashed clear hot water on it from another bucket. This kept any residue from leaving a streaky film. He repeated the rinsing process half a dozen times, using a squeegee on the windows until they glistened brighter than the paint. Finally he mopped all surfaces with a dry chamois, rubbing and polishing the two wads counter-clockwise to buff the finish into an even dryness. Then he emptied the pails, hung the cloths on the line, and went into the kitchen for a cup of coffee and a cruller.. By the time he had finished the car would be dry enough to wax.

The yellow brick felt like some giant raw diamond in his hand. Bruno palmed it and kneaded it back and forth for several minutes before it was usable. Then he pummeled it with a fresh piece of jersey until he had gotten the cloth up into a soft paste. At last he was ready to put the shine to the car, the moment to which all the dusting, sweeping and washing had been leading. He began laying on the wax, at first with long, hard strokes, then with shorter touch-ups, rotating the jersey until every square inch of the maroon-colored surface was covered. He had to stop frequently to knead the brick into its proper consistency. When he finished, Bruno was surprised to find that the beeswax looked as smooth as when he'd begun.

He buffed with cheesecloth, being careful to keep fifty thicknesses of cloth between his hand and the surface. Immediately Bruno knew he had gotten onto something.

The paint glowed thicker and deeper than when Mr. Biderbeck had brought the car home from the showroom. Growing more excited with every swipe of his hand he worked fast, shining at the surface until the car came alive in the daylight. Then it was done. He stepped away and spent a full five minutes looking at the Duesenberg. Mr. Biderbeck would be pleased with his work.

Thinking about the car didn't help Bruno's nerves. Rather, the idea that it came close to being dented in those narrow alleyways only made them worse. Besides, the smell of tobacco always made it hard for him to breathe, and the heat from the fire only made it worse. Alone, that was it. Bruno didn't like being alone. He'd been alone when he met Mr. Biderbeck. That was when he was in jail at Oran. He never knew why he was arrested; he was just trying to handle his own business like always. But a man and a woman got in his way; they kept asking questions about his route, about where he went and where he came from. They made him take them to his truck parked out on the street. But then they kept asking questions. He had to do *something*, so he put one arm around the woman to keep her from screaming while he choked the man with his free hand. She kept trying to scream, biting the ball of his palm, and he knew he would have to kill her. So he just tightened his arm until her neck snapped, and she died with her lips still rounded to the scream. He put their bodies in his truck and when he was on his way to Algiers, he pulled off and dumped them into the Mediterranean. He never figured out how the authorities got to him, although when he was arrested it seemed reasonable to him at the time that people had seen them together with him at the bar—and people will talk. But then he had killed another man a few years earlier, so he wasn't too surprised at going to jail.

They put him into a room without a light bulb, so that when dusk came outside his only window he knew he would spend the next twelve hours in darkness. Groping about until he could get to sleep wasn't too bad, but around ten o'clock the rats arrived—big ones, judging from the sounds they made. Sometimes their clawing and scampering kept him up for hours and he'd finally have to get up and pace about. One night they bit him on the legs, drawing blood. When he swung at them with his fist they only clawed him away, which infuriated him. He tore the bottom legs off the bed and, using them as clubs, smashed about the dark room until he couldn't hear any more noise. In the morning his table and chair were splintered and the walls were gouged, but he could find only one dead rat that lay broken and much smaller than he would have thought, in one corner of the wreckage. They wouldn't give him a new bed after that, so he had to sleep on the floor. The rats came every night. Sometimes he could feel them starting to crowd on him in his half-sleep. After a few months of that he lost his nerves completely. Then Biderbeck came. He never did find out why Biderbeck got him out; but he never really got his nerve back either.

He poured an extra finger of Scotch in the glass and added two ice cubes. If he was going to be alone the time would go quicker with a few drinks. He took a sip. It was good; real nutty flavor. Biderbeck liked straight Scotch. He checked his watch: 12:10. Then he noticed the frayed edge of his shirt. He would have to talk to the upstairs maid about that; too much starch in the wash kettle.

Suddenly the air was cold. It was after midnight, time to put more wood on the fire. He picked up a couple of birch logs and, twisting them in half as if they were twigs, threw the pieces on to the grate. He put a record on the Victrola—

Biderbeck's music all sounded the same to him— retrieved his glass from the mantle, and was about to take another sip when the chorus was cut across by a metallic *"wrright-wrright."* Probably a broken needle. He peered into the Victrola but everything looked all right there. He lifted up the needle arm. Just then he heard it again. This time it came from the floor. He tracked the rug and there, by God, there was the snake! Silver grey, coiling and sliding at a weird angle across the room. He couldn't believe it. He had to catch himself for a moment, and was almost glad not to be alone. Then he checked. The damn thing was coming right at him!

All business now, Bruno slipped the poker from the scuttle and, swinging it in short, awful arcs, smashed the snake into the floor. *Spwoing!* The coils exploded in a flurry of springs and wheels. Bruno was startled. More curious than frightened, he bent to pick up his quarry. Somebody was slipping it to him. He'd killed a bunch of motor parts in a snakeskin. Well, it wouldn't bother him any more. He swept everything up and threw the mess into the elephant's foot basket near the grate..

Then it started all over again. Another sliding, another metallic scrawl, this time louder and more insistent than the last. Bruno chucked the last bits of metal from his first kill into the trash, scanning the floor for the newcomer. Ah! There it was, slithering out from behind the liquor cabinet. This time he was ready for it. He grabbed the poker and stalked the buzzard, the anger in his eyes flashing mightily. Abruptly the snake stopped to raise its head. Bruno tensed, dug the balls of his feet into the floor and swung from his ankles. The poker's hook caught the snake at the base of the neck, sending its head into the wall with a loud *"whap."* The motor whirred a few times as Bruno bent to collect the remains of his kill.

Like all murderers, the task of killing gave Bruno the proper edge. His anger at being alone dissolved into a colder, harder logic. He swept through the room and out into the hall, methodically probing the poker behind curtains and into corners. His blood was up and his breathing whistled in the darkened room.

But all was quiet save for the oak log which popped and sizzled, burned half through with sparks.

He probed into the darkness beyond the library and was about to throw the light switch when he heard it again. *Wrright! wrright!!* Soft, then slow. Then again, and again. It was behind him, going away. Quickly now he stepped back into the study, just in time to see a new snake cut an angle not three feet in front of him. It looked so small, so helpless. He bent down, holding the poker like a driving rod and, reaching out his free hand, picked it up. For an icy second he felt the thing rotate in his fingers, watched it as it slid up his arm, felt it throb. There was something different about this one. Then he saw a small motor taped to its back and in that same half-second watched the snake open its jaws, pounce and . . . aaah, it had him!

He threw the poker into the fire, the thing on his other arm just a blur. Then he raged, stumbled, thrashed his arm into the couch, but he couldn't shake it free. The fangs were in his arm, probing muscle to bone. He swung again at the wall, roaring an outraged groan. Now it was off, and even as he was clutching his arm he stomped and kicked the gyrating thing on the floor until it was limp. But he didn't panic. He grabbed a dirk and slit his coat up to the armpit. In a second motion he sliced his sleeve. He could see the puncture marks now: two black dots hot to his skin. He slid the blade over them, cut again, and drew blood.

He took a pull, tasted bitter salt and spit out the blood and venom. He took another pull, tore off his tie with his free hand, and twisting it about his upper arm, used the dirk to tighten the tourniquet. His arm was already getting numb. He would have to get to the doctor quickly. The phone was on the desk. He couldn't remember Krakauer's number; he would have to call the operator. He grabbed the receiver, his mind racing with the things he would have to remember, fighting to keep out the confusion. He jiggled the receiver with his good hand. Silence. He jiggled it again. The tone started to come on. Then there was a tremendous rush that ground into slowness. Doors closing slower, slower still. The rush stopped. Nothing.

The heavy man fell back ever so gently from the desk, his last flickering thoughts not anywhere alert enough to register the instrument of his death which had penetrated one ear, and was now protruding out the other. Neither arrow nor bullet—it was a compressed golden snake, beautifully ornamented, beautifully lethal. Small drops of blood were already seeping from his wounds as he touched the floor.

Of course it was Phibes! Anton Phibes, pleased and powerful now, swept the room with one final, time-sharpened inclusive look. He noted that Vulnavia had reclaimed even the tiny jeweler's springs that were part of the motor propelling the mechanical snake, signaled his satisfaction to the girl and, his hands brushing the edge of his cape, escorted her from the room with the triumphant air of a great virtuoso.

Indeed, there was much to make the ubiquitous doctor proud. A scant week earlier his home, the fabled brownstone on Maldine Square, lay in ruins, its magnificent furnishings dispersed under the auctioneer's gavel, the proud portraiture of the Phibes' lineage sequestered in some mouldy artists' shops; his library, including his collection of Galen, Marcus Aurelius, Hermes Trismegistus and Dean Swift, defiled. And his laboratory, containing equipment built and assembled over decades of painstaking effort, and the data gathered from hundreds of irreplaceable experiments—all of it cindered, blackened, ground into the mud that lay thick over the scattered remnants of the House of Phibes.

Anton Phibes would have, could have taken vengeance. His last contact with the public authorities had not gone well. When he was in the Foreign Service he had learned to deal with the mid-and upper-echelon embassy personnel, and rather successfully at that. In fact, Phibes was making a name for himself as a hard-bargaining career diplomat who knew the subtle pressure points of foreign trade agreements. His genius, which had produced a series of published observations on the Red Bands of Mars, as well as his Covent Garden appearances where he conducted his own twelve-tone compositions, had always been tempered with a measured, methodical approach to whatever interested him; there were no surprises in Anton Phibes' life. His wife's death changed all that

Death in its inevitability confronts all men, and in their responses, men have roamed the boundaries of grief, indifference, and religious exaltation. For Anton Phibes, whose mind was honed to the precision of a mathematical formula, who ruled his life with automatic finesse, the death of his wife was unthinkable. Already past forty when they met, he was a polished man of parts who enjoyed—in the obscurity afforded him by an aggregate of successful investments that identified the House of Phibes with old wealth—the freedom to pursue his interests wherever they carried. Wealthy in her own right, Victoria was twenty two, and beautiful enough to be in demand in the literary salons of London and Paris. No one knew Phibes; everyone knew Victoria. Their love affair occupied the society pages for six months, drawing torrents of paragraphic excesses from the grimly attentive ladies that write those sumptuary columns. Their wedding made the literary pages, and the match that was damned by her family, dismissed by friends and lionized almost everywhere else, was launched in a newsprint benediction that culled Ovid, Dante and the fervid Troilus for its praise and predilection.

After that it got better. The couple travelled everywhere, were seen everywhere. Phibes was handsome, had great style and emerged as a great catch for the dashing girl. He adored Victoria in public. In private . . .? But who was there to know? All that one could observe— his gifts to her, the receptions, the excitement whenever they were seen together—conjured up something rare, something exotic.

Anton Phibes was in Switzerland when his wife died. He had concluded a trade agreement and was arranging details for a metals resources mission. Victoria had stayed in London to do some shopping. She planned to meet him when he finished and motor to Florence. By the time the call caught up with him Victoria was in surgery, Phibes had to hold himself back from shouting over the phone. The nurse was so damned cold, so matter-of-fact. He was already tracing the route he would take from Bern to Calais before he hung up. If he was lucky he could make the midnight Channel boat. The Hispano-Suiza was kept tuned and ready. He wouldn't stop to pick up his clothes; the only decision left was the route. South through Lausanne meant catching the heavy Paris traffic at dark. The northern route could be avoided in Paris, but it got quite winding after it left Basel.

He thought he could save an hour on it, and was on the road travelling north to Basel ten minutes after he took the call from London. That choice almost cost him his life.

It happened just outside of Epinal. He had made it to that famous military town in less than two hours, but lost an extra twenty minutes fighting the heavy produce carts that packed the streets. It was market day, and it seemed that every farmer for a hundred miles around was in town that morning. Traffic thinned out as soon as he left the town and he floored the gas pedal trying to make up lost time. The road was straighter, a series of long cuts and reverses flattening into curves that were a driver's nightmare.

The Hispano-Suiza took one of these at sixty and kept right on going, finally stopping a few hundred yards from the elbow by plowing into a rock and hedge field boundary which did little damage to the car, but thoroughly wrecked a grandiose beehive that the local honeybee population had labored on the for the past dozen summers. All Phibes remembered of the crash was the droning of displaced bees who were busy venting their anger on the rabbits, field mice, pheasants and other inhabitants of the hedgerow, killing everything that got in the way of their frantic dronings. Luckily he was upwind of the carnage, even luckier when the fuel tank, superheated by the sun's rays, parted at the seam, sending out a stream of benzine down the drive shaft, where it came in contact with the exposed spark plugs. The resultant explosion triggered an even larger eruption of the fuel tank, the force of which blew the car in half and sent the unconscious Phibes sliding into a small stream bed.

When he emerged from his coma a month had passed, and he was without identity. When the Hispano-Suiza left the road he had been thrown clear, skidding face down through the gravel and shrubs for a sufficient force and distance to mutilate his features beyond any possibility of repair. His nose, mouth, ears and throat were gone, literally torn from his face. And yet he lived. Skin grafts protected the deeper tissues of his face. Tubes, bandages and ointments allowed the torn surfaces of his frame to heal, form scars, and harden. Occasionally the white shapes about his bed would mumble questions and ask him to respond by raising his hand; or they would tap his arms and legs, or adjust the tubing that led into him. But he ignored the questions, the taps, the carbolic acid-reeking shapes. They didn't seem to matter; nothing seemed to matter except getting back to Victoria.

They didn't tell him on the phone why she was in the hospital and Phibes had never seen his young wife sick; he couldn't think of her as being sick, but there was a purity, an alacrity about that single telephone call that disturbed Phibes, that started a shift of the balances in his life, the momentum of which was to run a hard course.

He moved through his own recovery in a sort of frozen lifelessness, saying nothing, hearing nothing. Bandages were replaced, casts were refitted, tubing and bottles were changed, and finally removed. Presently his meals were brought in on a tray and the blinds on the window to his room were left open a few hours each day. Books, papers, and an occasional flower were left at the bedstand. He noticed that it was spring.

Then he saw it. A brief note In the *Times* literary section. It was a short, rather appreciative review of a book of poems by Victoria Regina Phibes. Very excited now—he hadn't known that she wrote—he read quickly through the critic's observations, until he began to stumble over the words . . . "Hers was a fresh young talent" . . . his hands were shaking . . . "grossly . . . and too quickly cut off." He checked the date.

Victoria had died over a year ago.

In the next instant he lost whatever sensations remained to him, the cumulative assault on his heart rate, breathing and other vital signs being so violent that he slipped into shock. His condition worsened over the next few days and the clinic's French doctors called in some specialists from the medical school at Basel in desperation. How their patient passed the crisis was beyond the reason of the assembled experts, but recover he did. Six weeks later Anton Phibes was discharged from the hospital, his identity still a mystery. With the bursar he left a note over his mark to cover the costs of his care. The bursar was reluctant to accept the paper, marked with an "X" as it was, until one of Phibes' attendants explained to his satisfaction that the patient was afflicted with a residual amnesia which would preclude much else.

Everything seemed righted a few days later when a bank draft made out in the amount owed was received from a Belgian bank. By that time Anton Phibes was in London, having put his "amnesia" to good use in the interim. He presently learned that his wife had died while still in the surgical amphitheatre, the obituary also noting that "Anton Phibes was killed in a fiery car crash while racing to be at his wife's side." It gave their approximate times of death as the same, and made rather mordant notice of this irony. Phibes, who already knew what he must do, now knew how to go about it. His recovery, in fact the entire balance of his life hung now on vengeance and retribution. It was the simplest personal logic that he would have to kill the men responsible for his wife's death, a logic that indeed carried him through every desperate crisis of his convalescence. The fact that he was legally—if not technically—dead, he would make good use of in the future.

It was Phibes who executed the seven members of the medical team and their nurse. It was Phibes who titillated the ghastly fancies of a sensation-loving public with the showiest sequence of deaths since Bluebeard. It was Phibes who arranged to confound, elude and disrupt every police scheme thrown up to prevent the relentless methodology of his crimes. And it was Phibes who left the field neither victorious nor defeated—but vanished before the eyes of the outraged authorities who had not managed even one glimpse of him, who wished they had never heard of him, and who wanted nothing better than to get him behind bars before his supple, resourceful mind could contrive the tenth and final course of the elaborate Biblical malediction he followed to woesome precision—the Curse of Darkness.

Indeed, there was much to make Anton Phibes proud. Five years after he concluded the G'Tach the murderers of his wife were, with one possible exception, all dead. In his flight from the authorities, he had made it impossible for them to take him alive. During the interval he had completed arrangements for a second phase of his retributive scheme: the restoration of Victoria's life. He'd learned of Akhenaton's Tomb, even acquired the left-hand segment of the Orisis papyrus which told of the River of Life contained therein. And now, despite the fact that his mansion was in ruins, and much of his life's work scattered to oblivion, Anton Phibes stood at the threshold of his fondest dream. The key to that dream, the detailed description of Akhenaton's tomb and all its approaches, was now in his possession. His hand tightened about the central segment of the papyrus that had been removed from Biderbeck's wall safe. He pressed it deeper beneath his cloak. Already a new excitement was beginning to return to the torn frame.

Chapter 4

When they finally got underway, Jonathan Biderbeck was in his cabin working. They were two hours and forty-five minutes late, which is what one would expect during the summer cruise season. Biderbeck had given explicit instructions to Lombardo to get their party to Alexandria as fast as possible. The travel agent came up with two other alternatives: a mail packet which sailed on the 24th, and a freighter which was taking a load of corrugated iron from Glasgow to Port Said. Neither could guarantee arrival time, so Biderbeck told Lombardo to book them on the "Empress of Quebec." Now he was disgusted at the incompetence of the cruise vessel, and cursing that fat fool of a travel agent for having gotten him on board in the first place.

To begin with, the pier was jammed with the most incongruous array of people Biderbeck had ever seen. Spinsters, tottering dowagers, displaced uncles, pudgy salesman types, and none of them was under forty. The men dressed in flowing capes, black hip boots and doeskin britches, and the women were awash in florid toga-like tunics. All pranced and preened about the two gangplanks in an orchestrated bedlam that bubbled into thunder as the morning's heat wore on. Every fifteen minutes new busloads arrived so that there were at least four hundred of these cloaked and gowned travelers on the pier by midday, and treble that number of interested relatives and friends. By then Biderbeck had learned that they were members of the Lord Byron League, off now on their decennial tour of the favorite Mediterranean sites of that fabled poet.

While the bedlam was still in full throat their luggage was mixed up. Pieces marked for storage had been loaded on board, and Biderbeck had to send Ambrose down to the hold to check on their removal so that the stacking order would be correct. Biderbeck was very insistent about it, because it was his practice to work while he was on the move and he had to know the precise location of his papers and equipment.

Then the staterooms were switched, with Biderbeck getting the cabin between Diana and Ambrose. The thought of enduring that sloppy, wheezing man in such risky proximity was so repugnant to Biderbeck that he ordered the porters to shift the hand luggage before he even stepped into the room. He slammed the door on them as soon as they were done, closing the inner stateroom door as well. Diana was showering and he knew that Ambrose was already into the gin and bitters. It had been a rugged start.

But the worst, the absolute worst was the loss of the papyrus. The expedition's success depended on that previous segment—and everything else depended on *that*. He had been furious with the police; they had been so damned diffident except for the one detective who kept commenting on Bruno's murder as if the man were a national hero. Bruno was dead, and nothing could bring him back. All the man talked about was preventive measures when he should have been concentrating on detection, and Biderbeck couldn't seem to get it through that the papyrus had to be found. He even considered putting in a call to Sir John Crow, who was then sitting on the Police Commission, but Biderbeck decided against it. There were too many details to attend to for him to get caught up in the futility of convincing a stubborn detective inspector of his responsibilities. Biderbeck sent a rather direct letter to the Commissioner, outlining his position in the matter, and left a few days later with the small confidence that Sir John's ire would filter down through the various division densities.

In all events the papyrus was missing, and there was little he could do about it. Advance camps, provisioning, crew equipment and the inevitable government licenses had all been set for weeks. The press and learned society journals had given the expedition their usual buildup, but Biderbeck had long since stopped caring about popular opinion. He couldn't NOT go; that was the point.

Besides, the model of Akhenaton's burial mountain was reasonably accurate. Constructed to scale by a team of architectural students, it drew faithfully from the papyrus, up to and including charting seven additional underground channels that had supposedly been dug into the mountain just before Akhenaton's burial to further thwart his enemies. But although he had copied the papyrus text, it contained a lengthy section on a hidden water clock, activated by valves, which Biderbeck felt was the key to the subterranean channel system. Without it they would grope around the dark canals for days, and perhaps miss the right one entirely. They had started late; they would be late finishing. It was a bad omen.

Biderbeck shuffled through three stacks of papers before he found his magnifying glass. He was working with a map of the Eastern desert which covered the span from the delta to the first cataract. It was an old Army field map and looked as if it had seen service with some subaltern throughout Allenby's campaigns. Biderbeck wanted to be sure of the distance from Alexandria to Amarna. They were going in by truck and their fuel capacity was limited enough as it was. He bent close with the glass: one hundred eighty kilometers. They would make it in a day with any kind of luck, and the two fuel tankers already allocated should be enough.

"Jonathan, you've been locked in with your charts since we left the harbor. It's already dusk and I found myself getting worried about you." Diana stood in the doorway. She had put on a flame-orange gown of scarf silk and already seemed very much at home on the ship. Biderbeck was delighted because this was the girl's first trip outside of England with him.

"I do neglect you, don't I? Forgive me."

"But why must you? It seems that ever since that horrible accident . . . when I was put in your care . . . that you've been *searching*. When I was ten you were off to China. That year in India when I was fourteen . . . Two years ago you did take me with you for a short visit to that wild island."

"Skellig Michael!" Biderbeck started to laugh.

"Jonathan, maybe I was too young, but I never did find out what brought people to that place. It was so forlorn, so lost, stuck out in the Irish Sea like that."

Biderbeck got up, kissed her, and brought her with him into the room. "You're too generous for words. The Romans started it all. After they gave up the ghost in Britain the land reverted to native rule—not that the Romans had improved things much. During the sixth century when the Eastern European monastics were on the move, a small band set out for the farthest outpost of Western Europe. They found the native British as inhospitable as the Romans had left them. Faith, and the fact that they had run out of supplies brought them to that tiny stand off the Irish coast. They had to wait another century before it was safe enough to come out." He kissed her again, his voice much softer now. "This time we'll make a real trip."

"But why? You have honors enough for a dozen men, and wealth enough for your needs, yet you're always seeking something that seems to elude you. You're SO mysterious at times."

"I? Mysterious?" Biderbeck felt obliged to sound puzzled. "I have my work. I like to think I'm somewhat necessary to certain people. To you..."

"But no one knows you, Jonathan, not even I—I really don't know what your life was like before the day we met. Not even when or where you were born." She pulled away from him and stepped to the porthole, looking out at the dark sea for a long moment. When Biderbeck spoke again, it was with almost noticeable relief.

"What difference do dates make? Should we dismiss our feelings merely because I'm a few years older?" He waited for his question to sink in, then answered it. "Of course not, that is, we're still breathing, still..."

Diana had picked up an old photograph from the open record file, and was looking at it intently. "But a girl is curious. I mean, I don't even have a photograph of you—there aren't any. Just this sort of thing taken on one of your expeditions. And, from the looks of it, this was snapped before I was born." She didn't seem at all troubled by that incongruity. Her worldliness was absolutely devastating.

"How do you do it, darling? You don't look a day older there than today." She said it almost like a challenge and, as always, it got to him. He touched her arm, brought her closer, kissed her on the chin, then caught himself. "You keep me young," he breathed, holding her away, "but you're right. I am neglecting you, and I'm sorry. Why don't you take a few turns around the deck? I'll find you in a bit, and we'll go into the salon and I promise not to talk about anything except the girl who is with me."

"I give you ten minutes, no more." She was out the door as softly as she had come in, shutting it with such grace that he would have hurried even if he hadn't planned on it. As always, Diana was going to have her way with him.

He went into the compact washroom to shave. It was another one of his eccentricities, a small edge of pride at looking fresh wherever he went. The room was the first part of the trip that really pleased him, all stainless steel and well-fitted heavy glass and marble edges. He zippered open his oilskin toilet bag and took out the wooden mug, brush, and razor with great care, then drew a full bowl of steaming water. He splashed his face, working his fingers into the skin. Then he rinsed the pig bristle brush, cleaning it until it was supple and ready to pat into the lather. He'd put a new limecake into the bowl before they left against the chance that the hard water might use up the soap faster than usual.

He shaved twice, the second time stroking against the grain. Then he rinsed with clean water, shaving a final time with the wet blade to catch the few tiny spots he had missed. He ran hot water into the bowl at full force; he couldn't stand the sight of soap scum. He turned off the spigot only when a dull glitter had been restored to the stainless steel. Then he patted himself with a few splashes of bay rum, combed his hair, dabbed himself with the towel, put his shirt back on and was just fitting the second cuff link in when the wall clock started to chime: eight o'clock. He was right on the button.

Biderbeck poked under the bed's heavy gray military blanket, sliding the stiff leather satchel out upright, taking care not to tip it over. He placed it, still upright, on his work table and was about to unstrap the top when he remembered that both doors were still unlocked. He quickly bolted them, checking the outer hall and Diana's room to ward off any possible intrusions.

Immediately he opened the case and removed a small leather case, this one in hand-worked leather bound in brass. This had two smaller locks on the edges and a somewhat larger one in the center, all of them securing the two doors which constituted the front of the case.

Biderbeck fetched his key ring from his working trousers and opened the case with three separate keys. The interior, fitted like a formal presentation case, was in claret-toned velvet, containing two ground glass vials, each stoppered with a heavy nailhead glass, and a gold spoon.

He placed a single folded handkerchief on the table before the case, removed the vials, and stood them on the clean cloth. Then, working with extreme care, he rotated the nailhead on the darker amber vial until its groove perfectly fitted the groove in the vial's tip and, tilting it at a measured angle, decanted three drops of the liquid contained therein into the gold spoon. He repeated the process with the second vial, paused for a moment to look at the viscosity caught in the base of the spoon, and swallowed the mixture. Then he rotated the nailheads on both vials until they were airtight, restoring them and the gold spoon to the case. Both vials were almost empty.

The entire process required less than ninety seconds. Biderbeck put the case back into the satchel and took out a small notebook, its thick pages covered with notations. Then he thumbed through the book until he came to the last page.

On it was registered his previous entry: "Elsinore Castle, December 31, 1926. Administered six drops." Five years ago to the hour! Biderbeck just had time to record the current entry when a loud knocking at the door broke the silence. Moving very quickly, he replaced the notebook in the satchel, strapped it shut, and slid it under the bed. Then he opened the door to his caller who was, of course, Ambrose, grown anxious that they would miss the buffet supper scheduled to start in just forty minutes.

"Jonathan, a locked door?" the big man hung precipitously in the doorway, his jowls expectant.

"A locked door against all eyes but yours, Adam. You're the only man I want to see. All squared away?"

He lumbered in, enjoying the intrigue. "Perfectly. And we're invited to the Captain's table, I hear. Care for a whiskey first?"

"We have time. I was working on some new approaches to the inner burial chamber. All but one of those corridors were meant to mislead, of course. I was thinking that if we entered from the south, that is, closer to the riverside . . ." Biderbeck glanced at the wall clock. "I'll show you on the model. Should we go to your cabin?"

Ambrose raised his palm. "Oh, I'm afraid I had that put with the other stuff in the hold. Didn't realize we'd be so occupied. Matter of fact. . . ."

"I can ring for the steward."

The stout man was already moving toward the door. He wouldn't dare risk Biderbeck's entertaining the shred of a doubt about his dedication. "Wouldn't think of it. The bloody steward would probe around for a couple of hours. Be back in a jiffy. In the meantime, you might order me a whiskey and a splash if you don't mind."

Ambrose hustled down the steel gangway, chuckling to

himself at his own fast stepping. Now if it had been the ballroom, and that girl he had seen at the shuffleboard that afternoon was on the reception line . . . well, that was another matter. The way she fit those white shorts *really* was another matter—and redheads always were his ruination, ever since he had been trapped in the closet with the vicar's daughter at Harrow. He was in the sixth form. Big for his age. But she was big for her age, too. The jugs on her were big enough to make any man and boy glad to be alive. Then there was Edith, sweet Edith, the research assistant in graduate school. Not much in the face department, but her legs were something else again. She used to haunt him on the field trips to Beachy Head. Bent over double, she did, digging for mussels with the whole class right behind her and anybody that wanted to could look all the way to kingdom come. But he always suspected she was holding it out for Dr. Frothingham, even though the old goat was in his dotage. Yes, it was redheads who kept him stepping.

Now Biderbeck was a different case. The man carried on like he was obsessed. He worked like a demon and played like two of them. Never did he see the man relax. Even at the track, which they went to regularly, rain or shine, on Saturday afternoons, Biderbeck was more controlled than the bloody books. He had all his picks in advance although he claimed he didn't spend more than an hour on the sheets. Of course you couldn't believe that because Jonathan Biderbeck had a fantastic percentage. Never got shut out. Most days four or five winners. With a few eights thrown in for good measure. But the man didn't really watch the horses. It was the odds board that drew his eye. That he watched like a hawk, placed his bets two minutes before post time, and usually collected. Used to drive him up the wall until Biderbeck consented to let him in on his secret. Hit the second favorite heavy, and play the favorite for a saver. But that's the way Jonathan Biderbeck was: methodical, precise—and he didn't like surprises.

Ah, there was the steward now. He wondered if the blighter would pull himself away long enough from those Lord Byron biddies to go down to the hold with him.

"Mr. Ambrose, we're out late, aren't we? Snack time starts in thirty minutes."

The man sounded like a bloody bird. Never could trust a pansy. He thought a quick minute about going down alone, but that would take too long. "Mr. Amalfi, glad I found you. Must go down below to fetch a model of one of the campsites. Mr. Biderbeck needs it instanter."

Amalfi pursed his lips and whispered to the half a dozen women he'd been entertaining, then he took Ambrose's arm. God, he was a greasy bastard.

After much clucking and chirping the unlikely couple, Ambrose a mountain of ill-contained bulk, and Amalfi, slight and slithering but still impeccable in his white day uniform, managed to negotiate the increasingly devious, increasingly narrow walkways within the hold.

Once there Ambrose was glad he had persevered with the steward, because he never would have been able to find his way through the forest of bulkheads, airlocks, and hatch covers. But Amalfi was a wizard, leading the heavier man through his paces as a terrier to a Saint Bernard.

One last hatch and they were in the proper storage locker, a pretty roomy place judging from the sound of their footsteps. Now he could hear Amalfi sniffing around in back of him. What the hell was that pansy doing? He cupped his fist. He'd swat the bastard if he tried any funny stuff.

"Eureka," Amalfi pirouetted near the light switch, "let's look in here."

He threw up a tarp and out popped a bunch of busty cuties. What was he trying to pull? Then Ambrose saw that the steward had got his signals crossed. The "girls" were nothing more than a bigger-than-life display advertising Mulholland's Gin. Drank it himself when he could get nothing better. They were models, all right: big flower pots, big lips, big tickets; a regular tit garden. Ambrose wanted to whistle, then thought better of it. He didn't want to offend the Ganymede after the little fellow had gone to all that trouble. Besides, it tickled him to watch Amalfi hop around all that cheesecake. "Mulholland's Gin is my Gin;" "Have a Gin with Ginger." Not that he'd mind two or three. "Sip a Little in the Clover." Now *that* was a hell of an idea. And that one was half out of her pants! Reminded him of dear, sweet, Edith, except the panorama was better. Rear end big as a Manchester Mallet. Must've been a true redhead.

"Dr. Ambrose, sir, will these do?"

Ambrose forgot about the weasel—but there he was, standing between two of the Mulholland Girls who were wearing crescent-shaped golden signs over their jugs. Something Arabic was written on it. "What's that you've got, Amalfi?" Ambrose was ready to get on with it.

"Your models, Dr. Ambrose. You're one of the advertising party, aren't you?"

Now it was coming clear. Behind the girls Ambrose could see rows of bottles ranging in size from magnums and jeroboams to gigantic, man-sized tots that looked big enough to hold enough of the Mulholland product to float the most gargantuan of receptions. "Well now, d'you think I wanted one of those up in my room?"

Amalfi was puzzled.

"Or that cupcake over there?" Ambrose pointed to "Edith," who had really caught his fancy. The steward actually started to blush.

"But you *are* with the advertising party? Opening a new territory in the Middle East. Parched earth. Bringing the blessings of good English gin. New bonds of friendship through trade. You *are* with that group, aren't you, Doctor?"

Amalfi had stopped fluttering. He looked crestfallen. Could he actually have mistaken a passenger? Ambrose decided to set it all right.

"My good man, you were close, but not there by a half. I am with the party of Jonathan Biderbeck. We *are* going to the Middle East, but I'm afraid on a somewhat different purpose. Scientific expedition. One of several such illustrious excursions Mr. Biderbeck has organized to advance our knowledge of antiquity. Can you keep a secret?"

Amalfi brightened at the hint in Ambrose's voice.

"We're after the last resting place of one of Egypt's greatest Pharaohs that may lead us directly to the tomb of Akhenaton. Now, do you know why that's so important?"

The steward shook his head. He didn't look as if he was quite with it. Ambrose warmed to the moment.

"Because Akhenaton was one of a kind. An heretic. An apostate to the State church. A mover and a shaker. Married the most beautiful whore in the land, he picked up his palace lock, stock and barrel and set up house a couple of hundred miles away. Brought about twenty thousand folks with him. Everyday people like yourself who were tired of the way things were going. And d'you know what they did?"

Amalfi was hooked, his face a positive blank.

"They made a go of it. Had a good time for about twenty years. And they knocked him up."

"Sir?"

Ambrose laughed. "Oh, not what you think. Sent his old mother down from the former capital. Thebes, it was. She harangued the poor king so he quit his wife. They lived separately for awhile, but it was no good. The old girl had him by the balls."

Amalfi winced.

"Had him by the old cullions, they did. He finally packed it in and went back to Thebes where they really gave him a going-over. But Akhenaton didn't have anything left to fight with. The buzzards had taken away his twat!"

Amalfi was starting to pull at his collar. Time to let him go. "Which is enough to push any man. I say, would you be good enough to show me Mr. Biderbeck's section before you leave?"

The steward cleared his throat and pointed to another cluster of trays. "Will that be all, sir?"

"Yes, Mr. Amalfi, and I do thank you."

The little man, a bit shrunken now in his still-pure whites, pivoted and was gone before Ambrose could bid him goodnight.

But it was good riddance. Certainly wouldn't do to have the bugger nosing around. You never could tell about the help on these holiday cruises. Shifty fellows. Light-fingered gigolos in it for what they could grab. Like dear Mrs. Chelmsford, the barrister's wife. Widowed not half a year, she left, on the advice of friends, on a world cruise to set her mind straight. Her first postcards from Gibraltar were all bubbly; apparently the lady had found a new lease on life. Three weeks later she was back in London sans luggage. The whole story didn't come out until much later. The entertainment director had cleaned her out—jewels, clothing, the entire set of new suitcases. He had even gotten the Chelmsford securities, which the poor woman had foolishly brought along on the cruise because she didn't trust the banks. The bastard had talked her into opening one of those cultural coffee shops in Chelsea. They went ashore in Istanbul to scout for the furnishings. One midnight he went out for a walk and never came back. Never trust your friends and your enemies will take care of themselves. Carried him this far, it did, and he guessed he could get by the rest of the way on it.

Ambrose found the cartons and cases under the tarp Amalfi had indicated, all neatly stacked and numbered. The model was in either #7 or #9. He'd have to untie the tapes to get at them. Looked like a messy job. Maybe he had better rest a bit after all that climbing around.

Just then it caught his eye. Could he believe what he saw? That gin drinkers' dream chorus was enough flimflam for the evening. But a calliope? Here, in the hold of the "Empress of Quebec?" And the real thing, no less!!

By now Ambrose had lumbered over to that marvellous machine and was shifting about it much as a man used to walking surveys his first automobile. He could hardly believe his eyes. Dials, levers and valves studded the white enamel base into which were fitted an assortment of odd-sized drawers. The top, which towered above his head, was an outsized box surmounted by a thick gauze curtain. The curtain was slightly parted at one corner and from its darkened depths came a humming. It was too much for him. One quick look wouldn't hurt. He bent closer and could see the large sheet of glass beneath, very cold. That's it! The humming was a motor refrigerating the box for some reason or other. He pulled out his handkerchief and wiped the glass. Good lord, it was a woman! She looked real. She *was* real!

Then it hooked him—a tight, dry iron prong in his neck.

Vertigo? He had just had a physical. Maybe if he bent back up? He put his knees forward and tried. Really tried. There it was again. Tighter! Must've pinched a nerve. He would have to get back up on deck and see the medico. But he didn't want those Lord Byron creeps to see him like this, bent over like a beggar. He looked around—or tried to look around, and he felt it again, like a dart, somewhere lower. He was losing sensation in his back. He could just feel the sharp jabs like he was being measured with a set of calipers. His legs were trembling, turning to glue, running into the floor. He didn't want to fall. He tried to look around and saw a blur through his tears, a darkened shape.

He felt the pain again, and several times again, and he knew that it wasn't vertigo, wasn't a pinched nerve. Somebody was with him doing something to him in the silence, and he was too terribly tired, too terribly helpless to do anything about it.

He woke up with a feeling of immaculate, perfect weightlessness. He blinked. The tears were gone and he could see things quite clearly now. Everything was much the same as before he had passed out, except that another light was on, a strong bare overhead bulb; except that he could not move.

But he could see—and he could see that he was propped against a post, angled, like a haberdasher's dummy waiting to be dressed. He could also hear whatever it was that was working on him moving about behind him and along his sides. It was all very detached, very anesthetic.

Then the pain edged into him, growing. It was lower, somewhere much lower in his back. This time it was like a spatula probing along the tops of his lumbar vertebrae. Then it was inside, inside his spine. He felt his back go.

When he came to he was on the floor. He felt like a

giant Vaseline tube, or a tub of peanut butter. For a moment he thought that Amalfi had come back, jumped him and was getting ready to do something awful. Then he heard something heavy being shoved—or was it rolled—across the floor. It nudged him, banged against his sides. Now it was turning. Must be pretty heavy the way it sounded. Ah, the gin bottle. He was staring right down the length of it now. It was bigger than he was, and solid glass. Could have held fifty or seventy-five gallons. You would get one helluva drink out of that bucket!

Gloved hands were at the top twisting it slowly, very slowly, grinding it open. Somebody above him. He tried to look up but his neck wouldn't respond. No muscle. No tone. Like the rest of him, a sack of jelly.

The top dropped to the floor. Now he was moved, shoved, grabbed into the bottle. They were trying to put him into the bottle! "You bastard. You filthy murdering bastard!" He was shouting. Wanted to shout. Couldn't. His head was shaking, his mouth pumping, but no sounds came out. Now he had it! They were trying to finish him off. Get him into the bottle and do him in. Well, let's see if the bastards could get away with it. He'd get somebody down here quick enough.

The tears filled his eyes from the shouting but nothing was coming out. He could make out the bottle moving in a big slow arc around his side. It bumped against him very dully, then stopped. Silence.

His eyes filled again, with fear this time. There was something going on he didn't like. A heavy pulling pressure on his legs. Then a roller going over him. He heard his knees pop. Couldn't feel anything, just the "pop," like a dog chewing a bone. The squeezing continued. His thighs, belly, trunk. He was tussled, pummeled, pressed into shape like a tub of jelly. He *was* jelly! The bottle was up to his armpits—and then he was in it, being pressed into the glass receptacle like so much jelly. He wanted to shout. Knew he couldn't. He wept, really wept instead, and tried to get his arms out but it was no use. They were pressed down next to his sides and slid in quickly. His head was next. He fell, dropped heavily to the bottom. The bottle was much bigger than he was. He looked up the sides of the neck, a glowing green glass, and heard them screwing the cap on before he passed out.

It was just as well that Ambrose didn't see the rest. Phibes, as always in complete control, upended the giant display bottle onto a small dolly and loaded it on to a freight elevator. Three minutes later they were up on "B" deck, deserted at this time of night. Phibes, his cloak up against him now against the night air—they had barely left the Channel—checked both walkways for any late strollers, but most of the guests were up in the ballroom for the ship's first night out party. Most of the others were in bed after the exertions of getting boarded. Of course for Ambrose all of this hardly mattered. It mattered considerably less when the dolly was wheeled to the railing and lifted to a hard, high angle sending the gin—and him—into the sea.

Chapter 5

"But don't you think we should make one more circle, Mr. Biderbeck? After all..."

The captain of the "Empress" was beginning to show his pique. He cleared his throat silently, without opening his lips, the way highly technical persons are wont to do. Having a man overboard was no laughing matter. At the very least it would show up on his record—a record, he could have added, that was otherwise spotless save for its frequent commendations. He was proud of every one of his thirty-seven years of service. He wasn't about to hazard a blot for the likes of a peacock like Biderbeck, even if he was in the papers every other day.

"No need at all, Captain! Professor Ambrose is a fine swimmer and you said yourself we are in the main shipping lanes. If he did fall overboard, which I consider most unlikely, he's been picked up by now." Biderbeck was getting impatient at the captain's mulishness. The two men had been at it for an hour and a half. If this was the kind of indecision the company commanded from its personnel he would make it a point of taking his business elsewhere.

"But sir, a matter of a few hours more or less..."

"Could be priceless. You can't imagine how important."

It was an effort for Biderbeck to contain his temper.

Crewes, for that was the man's name, had to give it one more try. Maybe the light touch would work. "Those pyramids and sphinxes have been out there for quite awhile; they'll still be there."

But Biderbeck would have none of it. He drew himself forward a bit and stared straight at the captain who, a few inches on the short side of the two men, needed every brass button on his uniform to withstand the stare-down.

"Captain, Professor Ambrose was in my employ. I can speak for him. He would want us to proceed full speed and stay on schedule, and I insist we do so." He swept the hair back off his forehead, "Or must I send a wireless to Sir Malcolm Fraser, your chairman?"

He had hit upon the doxology Crewes understood best. At that point the captain would have been ready to abandon Ambrose and anyone else who might be groping about on the high seas. "As you say, sir. Very good, sir. Original heading forward Gibraltar. Full speed ahead."

Crewes was already moving toward the door when a face-saving utterance broke through his chastened exterior. "We'll continue to thoroughly search the ship, of course. As a point of interest, Mr. Biderbeck, did Professor Ambrose . . . how shall I put it . . . very often touch the bottle?"

He glanced back at Biderbeck but the man was bent deep into his papers.

At that point Jonathan Biderbeck might well have contemplated the facts instead of rummaging about those endless maps. His prize papyrus, the central element of the mission, was missing. His colleague of the past twenty-five years swimming about in the dark somewhere. Then there was Bruno. Poor, poor Bruno. And they were already late by nearly a day. Another man might have taken a second look at things, even thought of turning back. But not Biderbeck. Neither a gambler nor a worrier, he dismissed the circumstances, replaced the lead in his drafting pencils and worked on.

Diana, in the meantime, had gone to bed. She never worried about fate, it just seemed to favor her. School, friends, her work at the museum—all seemed cluttered with exciting things to do, fabulous people to meet. She accepted her marvellous looks, her talents, her social position and her enormously happy existence. So far the only dark spot had been her parents' death, but that was many years past. She had had to struggle to put it out of her mind. Nothing could bring them back. Besides, there was Jonathan, elegant, elegant Jonathan. Second father, friend, guardian, lover—he was the only man who could bring strength to her soul and a tremor to her hand at the same time.

It had been almost that way from the beginning. She was *afraid* of Mr. Biderbeck, that dark, authoritative man who had been her father's colleague and employer in a score of mysterious enterprises. She remembered the great flurry of preparations, the compasses, field jackets, binoculars, and packets upon packets of leather notebooks. It seemed to take weeks to get everything together.

Her job was to put a number on each item and check it against her father's master list. Then one day Mr. Biderbeck would come by, sitting tall and terribly distinguished in his open car. His man would ring the doorbell to fetch her father's satchels, which he would load on the luggage racks. Often Mr. Biderbeck would come in. They'd talk a bit, her parents and the smartly uniformed visitor. Then her mother would serve sherry and they would all drink to the trip's success. Father never said goodbye, just tipped his cap as he walked down the front stairs. But Mr. Biderbeck observed all the courtesies, and he always gave her a little gift just before he left.

When her parents died it was natural that she go to live with Mr. Biderbeck. From the beginning he made her feel like a young lady—a very special young lady. He bought her wardrobe personally, selected her reading, arranged for her drama and music lessons, and consulted with her instructors on the progress of her work. When he was in London he took her to tea Saturday afternoons, after which they would travel by cab to different parts of the city, just to explore. She held his arm in public and he seemed very pleased when people mistook her for his daughter. Gradually her awe of the man turned to admiration. Heavier emotions soon followed, and on the eve of her sixteenth birthday she crept to his bed to be received, finally and at last as a woman, by the man she adored. Except for his travels, they had not spent a night apart since that time.

She thought of it now—the first time, the coolness of the sheets, the heat of her face and hands, the way their hair got tangled into each other's—and wished he'd come to bed. Very much she wished he'd come. Just before she went to sleep, she thought she heard the sheets part.

Another man who could, in fact did, consider the fates was Detective Inspector Harry Trout. Ever since the Phibes murders, Trout was known as the man who had a way with the bizarre. In fact, Trout had earned a reputation as being somewhat shrewd even before his encounter with Doctor Phibes.

Young, resourceful and hard-nosed beyond his years, Harry Trout suffered from too much success too soon. Promoted Inspector before he was twenty-four, Trout found evidence and won convictions where all others had failed. He was in a hurry; he stepped on toes; he got results. After his resolution of the Darby spinster's case in which he was roundly accused of rough handling, the Operations Office assigned a watchdog to Trout in the person of Tom Schenley to keep the young livewire from further damaging himself. But even that phlegmatic war hero couldn't slow Trout down as a broken jewelry ring and the flushing out of a wretched chemist after a cycle of taxicab garrottings had made London housewives jittery soon attested. Not that Schenley didn't try. He brought the young man home and introduced him to his wife's cooking, which included a New Zealand trifle that first night at table. Trout was a black-coffee-for-breakfast type, and the Wednesday evening dinners, as artful as they were, were all but lost on him. Schenley had more success at sports where he got the youngster interested in handball, only to have the plan backfire when he found that Trout was getting to work an hour earlier just to play in the upstairs gym. Finally he tried women, but after running through a chorus girl, a seamstress, and a Latin teacher, Trout showed no signs of wavering. In fact, his work reached a new peak. He was sent out on a speaking tour of other municipal departments. In Liverpool they called him another Holmes; in the Midlands, "super-sleuth;" at home, considerably less.

But if Harry Trout read his own publicity, he didn't show it. Like Candida, be passed through his world of crime and criminals unperturbed, untrammeled, and unbesmirched.

Until Anton Phibes.

The spectre of eight unaccounted-for murders would have been a burden for any self-respecting professional. For Detective Inspector Trout it was an anathema.

After the case—"ordeal" was a better word—he retired into himself. He withdrew from even the limited world of his acquaintances. In conversation his speech, formerly staccato and to the point, became taciturn. He seldom said "hello," even to his superiors. He stopped playing handball. No longer did he carry his lunch to work, a brown bag neatly secured by rubber bands, tucked underneath his suit coat. He went out for long periods, was seen at free lunch counters, and even grew a modest paunch. His abstinence crumbled in other areas. He acquired the tobacco habit, wavering between pipes and cheap, foul cigars. He drank; not the usual porter, but whiskey in double shots and a pint for a chaser.

He dropped the chorus girl, who promptly spread the news that Trout had lost it in the sack! Some ignored her; others didn't, and shook their heads at the man's deterioration. He abused the little Latin teacher. She was seen at class wearing smoked glasses. She cried frequently and wrote long letters to her mother which were never sent. The seamstress was not at home to his calls, but that didn't bother Harry Trout.

He was said to frequent Soho—the seamier dives. Talk ran high that he had taken to café-brawling, chippie-chasing, or worse. Someone called him a sadist.

His activity reports were late. Sometimes they didn't come in at all. When they did, they tended toward the dilatory. It was wondered what he did with his time. Division Chief Waverly recommended a sabbatical: three months in Cornwall, or the Crime School at Uppsala. Others suggested that the detective go to America. Correspondence was sent out to the FBI couched in very official terms—very, very official terms. Talk was about an idea exchange; international cooperative front against crime; new techniques to fight the new wave; an Anglo-American partnership to solve the social disease. America would have none of it. It seemed they were satisfied with their own fighters—and their own crime rate.

The upstairs office wrung their hands. Harry Trout, once their best man, the pride of the Department and a public figure, had gone off the track. He slouched in the hallways, his speech was irascible, his reports turgid. On a case he could work with nobody, and none with him. He insulted everyone around him: visitors, suspects, colleagues, superiors. Once a standout, he'd become odd—and odd men go out.

He was put on notice. When asked if he understood the gravity of his circumstances, Trout merely grunted. Grunted like an old has-been, yet he was scarcely thirty. Six months went by and he grunted again. Within a year it had gotten worse. He moped. The Latin teacher returned his engagement ring. He breakfasted on eggs Benedictine and had his first eye-opener at nine thirty A.M. Light on the water. The months dragged, his reports lagged, his work stopped.

But crime went on. Men and women were set upon in the streets. Beaten. Robbed. Murdered, and murdering each other. Has-been hero or not, each police officer had to carry his load, or someone else would. It was bad to have a non-producer on your hands; bad for morale, bad for the Department.

Papers were drawn up; Trout was on the way out. It was time to give somebody else a chance. New blood, new courage. Waverly pleaded. It was not like him at all, but he did argue the man's case. At the last hour Trout was saved and given a safe new assignment. Not too much was required of him. Shore patrol; on the beach, that is, to stop the alky boats from landing.

Waverly was vindicated. Good man. Ought to be

allowed to make retribution. He called Trout in and gave him the news. He thought he saw a smile but there was no time for sentiment. He requisitioned a flashlight and a flare gun and sent the beggar off.

The roller coaster bottomed out for Harry Trout at Pegswell Bay. The fog levelled his head. The packed sand put firmness back in his stride. But it was a million-to-one shot that started him into his career again.

It happened about three weeks after he got to Margate, where he'd taken a room in one of the old summer hotels to get a break in the rates. His pockets were riding high those days, and even Trout knew that the paychecks weren't going to last much longer.

The day was Saturday. He got up about five in the afternoon, took a quick shave in his washbowl, and went down to the main floor dining room to grab a quick bite before he went out to work. He didn't mind working weekends because there wasn't a damn thing to do in Margate except to go to the picture show. Tuesday, his day off, was just as good a day to do that anyway. The cook was late so he killed time with gin and bitters. The beef and horseradish sauce was ready by the third drink but it was cold, so he just ate his biscuits and red cabbage and packed it in. The bus to Pegswell left at seven and it was a long, cold ride.

When he got there the sand was deserted as usual except for a bunch of dogs pattering around the dunes. Looked like a bitch in heat. Had all the Romeos in town after her, she did. He could see them brush up close and she running off at the last minute. A couple of the smaller ones got so excited they stopped every few feet and pissed into the wind, but it didn't seem to bother them.

He walked about four miles and the air was beginning

to get inside his coat. Good and clean and cold it was, too—and wet enough to make his underwear stiff. But he kept at a good pace and liked to hear the clam shells underfoot, so he didn't mind the fog. Every once in awhile he would turn around just to double-check, which he didn't like because his coat collar was rimmed with droplets which ran down the back of his neck when he twisted. It was the third or fourth time—he couldn't remember which—when he saw some goings-on way off down the other end of the beach. Looked like a big searchlight and some men milling about. He spotted the outline of a small ship just past the breaker line. He couldn't make out the business, but thought he'd just go and check anyway. He didn't think the smugglers were fools enough to come in lit up like a Christmas tree. Just the same he flicked the safety off his flare gun. It never hurt to be ready.

He ran most of the way at a good clip. Fast enough to nail some of the buggers he'd brought in, he laughed to himself. But his breathing stayed good, so he took his hands out of his pockets and scissored the air just to pace himself. About a thousand yards off he saw the Coast Guard helmets on the men on the beach, and was almost disappointed. The ship moved in now in front of the breakers, and kept reversing its engines to stay in place. Then he saw it in the water.

Trout got there just in time to see them haul in the bottle. It was the biggest damn bottle he had ever seen. The label said "Mulholland's Gin" but the thing had been floating a bit. He had a feeling that whatever was inside wouldn't be quite up to snuff.

He flashed his I.D. and the Coast Guard boys were good enough to give him the first look. Maybe they had seen it, too. Seen a bit more than him, maybe.

He rolled the thing up on the sand with the help of the lads. The outside was covered with seaweed and sand, so that you couldn't see too well through the glass—but something was inside. The cap screwed off only after he put his knee to it. It was stuck with sand which is why the damn thing probably floated. Then he bent down and stuck his light into the neck. There was a man inside!

"I'm a police officer, sir!" Trout had to check himself at the echo of his own voice. The Guard crowded around him now, eager to get a look. Trout called in again, but only for the formality of it. Then he turned to the ensign.

"Bought it. Get him out. Watch out for flying glass. But try to save the bottle if you can; we'll need it for evidence." It was getting good to him now, being in charge. While the men brought up a can of grease and a hawser, an ensign lit two cigarettes, offering one to him.

"Soon as I spotted it, thought I'd best call the local authorities. Glad you came by, sir, as our ship's radio is out and the nearest phone is back in Margate. Never seen anything like it. How do you suppose he crawled in, sir?"

"He didn't crawl in; he was *put* in." His voice was crackling with the old authority now. It felt so good he even hefted the light to emphasize the part.

"You don't say. What sort of madman would do such a thing?"

He was looking hard at the bottle now. The crew had gotten the rope about the man's chest. He was a big, fat, bulky chap, a little damp from the handling, but still intact, and dressed in a tuxedo. Odd. They were trying to get him out of the bottle without cracking it. Of course the grease helped. But it was still odd.

The ensign's question filtered through and tickled him in just the right spot, as it would later turn out.

It wasn't easy for Harry Trout to get back to London. Oh, there was enough interest in the bottle all right, but the case was turned over to a new rising light by the name of Cranmer, who came down and began making a nuisance of himself right off the bat. Trout was told to return to his shorewatch and "report anything suspicious!" Three weeks of it with that pipsqueak nosing around and he had had a bellyful. He called his old partner Tom Schenley, who agreed to let him hide out in his office for a few days until they figured out where to go from there. Two hours later he was on the train, leaving the beach at Pegswell entirely undefended except for the presence of Cranmer, who seemed quite up to the task.

He went right to the office as soon as he got off the train.

He could get a room later, and after that dump down in Margate anything would look good. Schenley wasn't too happy to see him, but he warmed up after tea, had the "Man in the Bottle" file sent down from Records, and set Trout up in a corner of the small office to catch up on his reading. Tom had to leave on a call about three, and was surprised to find Trout gone when he got back.

But he was in the office the next morning at eight sharp; suit pressed, freshly shaved and ready to see Waverly. He had a file set up, and Schenley could tell from its colored stickers that Trout thought he was on to something. But it was Waverly's Embassy Day. The Division Chief had gotten quite important of late and had been spending one day a month at the various foreign embassies in his official capacity as Liaison Officer. Schenley suggested that he meet some of the new men in the division but Trout passed. He said that he had some more catching up to do, grabbed his file, and left. It was to be a fortnight before Schenley was to see his old friend again.

"Trout, I want you to keep in mind just one thing when you repeat what you said, and that is that I am your superior and still Division Chief, and that fitness reports are going in this weekend." They were in Waverly's suite which, Trout noted, had been remodelled. The grim green wallpaper had been overpainted with magenta enamel, fitting color for a devil like Waverly. The threadbare rug had been taken up, replaced by a nondescript fabric. It was green astonishingly enough, but it looked like a desiccated putting green. Waverly's hand could be seen in the wall decorations which consisted of his plaques, arranged in the same square-jawed formation as before. Nothing else had changed.

The two men had been talking since nine, after Waverly had kept Trout waiting in his outer office for an hour. It was now eleven.

"Keeping in mind the Yard's experience with Dr. Phibes, I do believe that Phibes is capable of anything, sir." Trout spoke slowly but with full determination. The file on the doctor had been closed for several years but he remained a touchy subject. For the Division Chief, the Phibes name was like a detonator cap.

"Including rising from the grave?" The smaller man was breathing smoke.

"I see what you mean, sir. But still . . ."

"Assuming that—only an assumption, mind you—on the assumption that your Doctor Phibes did somehow rise from the dead, did it ever occur to ask yourself how he could have gotten past British Customs? With that face?"

"That would be difficult, sir. Most difficult indeed. But adding everything up . . ."

Waverly did it for him. "A man in a bottle? A bit unusual, yes, but he was washed up in the Channel, now, wasn't he? I mean Pegswell is across from France. Did you think of that, Trout? A typical Frenchy kind of homicide, eh? Bizarre. Absinthe. Continental decadence. Got the picture, Trout?"

Trout tried another tack. "But taking into account as well the dispatch of Mr. Biderbeck's manservant..."

Waverly lunged from his seat. His face was redder than the walls. He did look like the old Lucifer. "Accuracy, Trout! Facts, damn it! Manservant who? What manservant are you babbling about?"

"The golden asp business. Bruno, sir." He put one finger to his ear and made a swooshing sound. He was on shaky ground now but he set his voice and got on with it. "I would describe that as typically Phibesian, sir. And since there are absolutely no clues, no other suspects..."

Waverly had recaptured the strength of his desk chair, where his rocking indicated that the interview was soon to be over. "Make a report, Trout, and don't bother me with will-o'the-wisps."

Trout struggled to salvage it. If he failed, he knew it was back to Margate.

"I have, sir. It's in the proper channels and should reach the interested parties soon."

"Then let nature take its course." Trout's hopes sunk several notches lower. He was frantically casting about for a saver when Waverly's secretary poked her head in the door and announced a Mr. Lombardo to see Mr. Trout. Trout cast protocol to the winds and asked her to show the man in. Mercifully it was too close to lunch hour for Waverly to notice the breach, other than with a few clipped questions. Waverly didn't even raise his head. He just sat there, removed two hard-boiled eggs from a center drawer and slowly cracked, peeled and consumed them in a gathering chorus of chews and swipes. Just then the flaccid Lombardo, arms and legs everywhere, head bounding like a jack-in-the-box, popped into the room, averting —Trout knew in his marrow—a volcanic counter-swell from the Division Chief. Waverly himself, who was still ruminating, could say nothing. Before his first words were out Lombardo had already got up steam, which was a fatal tactic with persons who talk much and say nothing.

"Inspector Trout, the plot thickens!" Lombardo tapped the door with his foot, and was inside in a rush.

"Aha, Mr. Lombardo, this is Division Chief Waverly, my superior."

"What's this all about, Trout?" Waverly swept the eggshells off his desk.

"Sir, Mr. Lombardo handled the passenger list of the 'Empress of Quebec' when she sailed last month." Trout was talking just to ease the situation, but Lombardo talked faster.

"A juicy divorce action. Jewelry, passion, all that. Oh, I remember that time the Duke of Covington took over all the suites on 'A' deck of . . ."

"Mr. Lombardo, I believe you said you might verify Professor Ambrose being on the 'Empress.' " Trout caught the agent in the midst of a gesticulation. He stopped, played the scarecrow, then started giggling.

"Ambrose? Who would have thought it? Still waters, they say." He unfurled a large crumpled list from one vest pocket, some pince-nez from another, and combined the two with some squints and chucklings long enough to start laughing. "Why, yes. Sold him the tickets to Alexandria myself. Wanted a stateroom near his friend Biderbeck." Then another thought dredged up and he got his arms moving again. "No! You mean Ambrose and that lovely Diana Trowbridge?"

Trout had to tap the man's chest for fear he'd engulf him. "Briefly, Mr. Lombardo, we want to find out if Professor Ambrose was acting strangely—if anyone strange was with him. Did he mention any enemies?"

Lombardo veered and started pawing. "Let me think. Well, he was always looking to go somewhere to dig up things. Bit like you, I suppose, but strange? Not exactly."

The wall clock inched into the noontime hour. Waverly saw a way to get rid of these fools before they thoroughly ruined his day.

"Lunch time, gentlemen. That will be all, Trout. And thank you for your help, Mr. Lombardo."

But the man didn't hear him, or he was mesmerized by the magenta decor. In any case, he went on.

"Not as strange as some I get. Oh, I get some dillies. Regulars, you know."

Trout attempted to take the travel agent's elbow, but the man quickly turned and was marching toward Waverly's desk.

"Mad. Weird. 'Can I take my four cats along?' 'Is there enough liver on board?' That sort of thing. 'Can I have a piano on board?'"

Trout overtook him and started applying a gentle pressure to his elbow, but still the torrent came.

"Pianos! That's not the worse of it! Talking about eccentrics, I had a chap who wanted an *organ* in his stateroom. Why, he went out on the 'Empress'; on Professor Ambrose's trip, as a matter of fact!"

Trout exchanged a quick glance with Waverly. He had heard it, too. He moved the still oblivious agent back into the room.

"Well, I suppose you have your crosses to bear too, don't you? All of us servants of the public . . ."

Trout wanted to pin him down. "An organ? Are you sure? Is he on the passenger list here?" He took the list from the man's finger and began scanning it. "What name did he travel under?"

"Ah, Schweitzer."

"Schweitzer?!"

"And an organ?" Waverly was coming around. Lombardo had found the name and was holding the list out for him to see.

"Here we are. Luigi Schweitzer. Mr. and Mrs. If you believe that, you'll believe anything. They're some kind of entertainers, far as I can make out."

"They?"

"His assistant. A girl. She made all the arrangements. Quite lovely. But another weird one. Dreamy. Another world." He got absolutely confidential, his voice gurgling into a whisper. The two policemen hung on every word. "You know what they do out there with the Bedouins and all. The things they smoke or puff? Well, I'm not surprised. Second time they booked the same accommodations. Went out once before, about five years ago. Must have made a hit. Took a lot of clockwork musicians. Never caught the act in vaudeville myself."

"She made the arrangements, you say? So you never saw his face?" Trout was back on the track.

"No, I never did. Dreadfully sorry."

And then it was over. "Thank you, Mr. Lombardo. We appreciate your help very much indeed."

Lombardo was fulfilled, a good citizen. His duty finished, there was time now for one bit of business. "Anytime at all. And you can trust me. Mum's the word. Never babble, never gossip. A pleasure, gentlemen." He dropped a card in each of their hands.

"And if you're ever thinking of a little jaunt, keep me in mind."

Trout waited until he was safely gone, then turned to the Division Chief.

"Sir?"

But the man was unmoved. "Looking for a free vacation, Trout? You angling to get a boat ride out to sunnier climes? Well, you better think again. You just walk back down to Margate, and I'll take the whole thing up in due course. Wild hypothesis, Trout. You haven't thought the thing through."

His intercom buzzer cut him short before he could dispatch Trout. Waverly took the call, stiffened, his voice becoming progressively grave. "Waverly here. Oh, yes sir! You did? You received the report? Yes sir, I'm right on top of both the Bruno and the Ambrose matters. Yes sir, a brilliant report by my man Trout. Helped him a bit with it, as a matter of fact. Followed through this morning. Wonderful lead. I see, sir. I agree. Yes, sir, I did want you informed instanter! Oh, I do, sir. Thank you, sir."

He hung up and looked at Trout, who didn't have to ask, but did.

"Was that . . . ?"

Waverly pulled back. "Matter of fact, yes. And listen, Trout. I've come to a decision about this Phibes matter. I've got the old man to give in to me as he usually does when he's on the start of something important. Ever been to Egypt? Thought not. Can't take time. We'll go out on a flying boat, RAF Calshot. Eighteen hundred hours, tonight. Right? Don't just stand there, man, get your tropical gear. Get cracking!"

He started to say it again, but Trout was very much gone.

Chapter 6

Ragusa! The name was curling around in his head like some damned bee drone. It had been there for a long time, like a bean in a coffee pot, a place you never went back to again. There *was* a town named Ragusa. He had seen it on maps of the continent, but had never been there. Sicily, that was it! Ragusa was a town in Sicily.

It started to come to him, then he lost it in another drone: a swaying, slipping hum in his kneecaps, elbows, and the nape of his neck; soft, drowsy vibes bounding their cottonball strokes along the various edges of his hand. Cushions of noise grown into murmurs. Old intrusions become malleable. Sound accommodated to the utmost. Hard edges, worn down, polished, lubricated in anticipation.

Waiting! He'd been waiting. That was it! He *is* waiting, waiting to get somewhere. He is going somewhere, on his way now. Getting there. Waiting to get there. That's the sound. Motors droning. They had picked him up. Harder, stronger then, they'd picked him up. It was like being in a big bathtub pulled up all of a sudden from its plumbing. But the lousy thing got them up off the ground. Put them out over the water which he didn't want to look at. So damn far down, flecked and frothed from one edge of the window to the other. Hey! Wait a minute! That wasn't the Channel down there. Too big and empty.

Then it came to him. "Came back" is more accurate. He had been dreaming. In fact, probably he had been dreaming since just after they took off. He was in a big wheat field, with stalks high as your shoulder waving down the slope for another half-mile until it ran into a hedgerow at the bottom. Behind the hedge was a pretty thick stand of trees which poured out a steady *cannonade.* Several batteries were in there; from the thickness of their shot he could tell something was in the works. He was with Picton's Corps and had marched with Wellington ever since the Peninsula. They were standing now just under the lip of the hill so the shot, instead of getting at them, was tearing up the hilltop. Great clots of earth had been uprooted, sending down a steady dirt shower which had gotten everybody filthy but caused no more damage than that. In fact, the bombardment was a tremendous waste of gunshot and a lot of bloody racket.

After what seemed like an hour the shelling stopped. The men used the lull to dust themselves off and a few brave souls walked up to the hillock to take a look, where they were promptly shot at but nobody was hit, thanks to the awful marksmanship of the French, which was no better, no worse than their own. He had just taken a nip from his canteen when the bugles sounded. High staccato brass blasts that could have blown the tops off the houses had there been any still left standing. Cadenced to the staccato came the larger sounds of the cavalry on the march; leather on leather of boot to hushed saddle; bright brass breastplates of the *cuirassiers,* the dragoons' stiff S-shaped plumes; and the horses—at least a thousand to the line—snorting and cantering, their hoofs trembling the turf, impeccably ordered, impeccably deadly.

They had been expecting d'Erlon's Corps ever since the runners came up with word that Hougoumont had fallen. The bombardment was just a preliminary. No one paid that much attention anyway because the shooting was so bad. The only artillery an infantryman had to be afraid of was grapeshot, and that was when he was attacking. All the rest was a lot of noise, an excuse for the cannon generals to strut.

But the cavalry was different, and the French, were about the best there were. Didn't the bloody Austrians get beaten by the cavalry at Jena? Murat had cut them up like a butcher going through a leg of mutton. The French came at you with the sword-point straight on and angled up; they didn't waste time slashing. If they got you, you were dead, because that kind of wound went in deep and bled a lot. Oh, they did a lot of shooting, too, especially the dragoons, who carried two or three pistols and a breech-loader. Once he got going a dragoon looked like a bloody squad, because he would charge in a little weaving motion and get off a blast each time he angled. But the hand guns were as bad as the cannons, so nobody worried too much whether the horseman shot all day or not.

You got the worst of it if he got on top of you. The damned horses were as big as wagons and specially trained to take a man down and kick hard. His old corporal had gotten it that way: he stood up to a charge too long and had his lungs kicked in. He walked off the battlefield and wouldn't go to the surgeon even though he kept coughing up blood. They found him dead in his cot a few days later. The only way to take on the cavalry was to kill the bastards before they got you.

Their own bugler was at it now and he could hear the

other chaps in the brigade moving in the wheat. Picton had put the Union Brigade in the dead center of the line. He had visited every position early that morning to see how the rations were going. It had rained all night and most of the men were just getting out of their soaked blankets when the General made his appearance. They were glad to see him — black boots softly polished, cloak and uniform turned out like he meant business — a picture of confidence. That was just what Picton wanted them to think even though he only talked about the cooking fires — was there enough dry wood about to get breakfast ready? He wanted the men to get set up because they'd be there for the rest of the day. As soon as the first fires were smoking Picton left, riding tall and graceful for a man of his years.

The main mass of horsemen was in the woods now where the batteries had been firing earlier. He could hear them coming through the bush and trees, stiff and full of purpose. He thought it would be good to have some sharpshooters downhill a bit, but no one had given the order and it was too late now. Here they came! The first line of lancers was coming out of the woods in almost perfect formation; then another row behind; then another.

The corporal gave them the order to form a square but it was automatic, because that was the only thing the infantry could do when they saw cavalry coming. His part of the line formed a "V" and then another, and the square was made. Then they fixed their bayonets and stood waiting, a double box of men in the hot wheat field.

Harry Trout saw the thing clearly now although he had never been to Waterloo; had never been to most places, for that matter. And it wasn't a dream at all, but sort of family war legend plugged into the Trout chronology by his great-

great-uncle Duncan Andrew Trout who had, indeed, acquired the highest military distinction amongst the Trouts for his presence at the Battle of Waterloo. Harry himself had been too young by a year to see active service in the Great War. It was left to his cousin, Fernley, to keep the family name unblemished in its patriotic exercise. Fernley Trout was one of Haig's aides-de-camp and had the distinction, if such can be said of it, of serving with the Commander in Chief from Paaschendaele to the Second Battle of the Marne, where some well-directed artillery fire had separated him from his left foot. Fernley spent the remainder of the war recuperating on the Trout family estate in Devon, with naught but harsh comments about the war's leadership in his absence. The few times he had gone down to Devon Harry had been privy to his cousin's declarations on the ills of trench warfare. The field commanders squandered their men and general officers were too far removed from the front lines to do anything but raise the stakes. Sixteen thousand men died in the opening assault on the Somme in 1916, with a few hundred square yards of mud to show for it. Anyone, even a rank amateur, could have done better. Wellington would have settled things in half the time.

After sitting mute through three or four of these tirades, Harry decided to do some reading on the subject. He didn't much like reading, being a bit too active for the book-and-easy-chair routine, but once he got into some thing he stayed with it. Histories, memoirs, battle plans—he read everything he could find on the Napoleonic campaigns. He hunted down personal correspondence and newspaper accounts from collectors, even making a special excursion to call on the great grandson of DeLancey Graham to avail himself of some of that illustrious quartermaster's correspondence.

He also started his own correspondence, at first with a

variety of personages in Spain, all of them dubious, to gather a sense of Wellington's strategy on that peninsula. Like Napoleon's military commanders—first Augereau, then Brune—he got nowhere into the subject past the fact of the Iron Duke's disdain of pitched battles. The war and its purposes in that area remained opaque to him. His efforts with the Russians bore somewhat better fruit. After eight months of inquiry he learned that (a) a group calling itself the Kuznetsov Society did exist, and (b) that it did possess the most complete account of the Grand Armee's eastward excursion ever amassed. He also learned that (c) the group did not grant outsiders the privilege of viewing these documents unless they were "acknowledged and accredited" scholars.

The ultimate sum conclusion of Harry Trout's excursion into his historic byroad was that Wellington was, for all intents and purposes, a clod, and that Napoleon should never—even if he had disposed of half the men assembled to his cause—have lost at Waterloo. That the facts were otherwise bothered him not half as much as that his family, particularly the rancorous Fernley Trout, disagreed with his reasoned and brilliant discoveries.

Just as the Calshot dipped its wings the name of the man whose titled appellation had started his dream came to Harry Trout. Auguste Frederic Marmont, like the illustrious Michel Ney and Louis Nicholas Davout, was one of twenty-three similarly gifted men deemed fit to wield the marshal's baton by Napoleon. Most were young men when they gathered to the Emperor's standard. Their efforts propelled France into a political and military preeminence that stirred the pride and envy of her contemporaries and the imagination of successive generations. After Waterloo some remained in the public eye, others returned to private life, and all attempted to weather the violent political tides now turned against them. One of the number turned informer. His name was Marmont, Duke of Ragusa.

The plane stopped for refueling at Malta, flopping to earth like an exhausted duck. Trout didn't have the heart to wake Waverly; he had been snoring since they left Biggin Hill aerodrome. He thought about hopping out for a pack of cigarettes, but decided against it. The plane was such a ramshackle affair that the less he saw of the outside of it the better. He would just have to string out the one pack he had stuck away in his flight sack, that is if it wasn't mixed in with his shaving soap.

The plane lurched a final few hundred yards, then sputtered to a stop. The propellers kept jolting some minutes afterward, as if they didn't want to stop for fear of not being able to start up again. Finally they gave up. Then a thud, then nothing. The door to the cockpit stayed closed. The front and rear hatches stayed closed. No one entered. No one exited. No one came.

The plane just sat in the middle of an empty concrete strip which stretched, apparently endlessly, toward the flight tower in the background. That, too, was deserted, or at least it looked deserted. Three flagpoles stuck up from its corrugated tin roof. He couldn't make out the identity of the flags but they were red and green and white, and they flew smoothly in the wind. Otherwise there was no motion about the building, which was the only sign of habitation around.

Then he heard it, the surging groan of a band. The *Marseillaise!* At first a strong thin line, then the heavier clash of cymbals, brass and drums; it was a military band. He could see it now, a mass of khaki advancing up the landing strip. What a blare! What a gigantic, filling sound! They came closer, playing the anthem on polished brass and agitated drum top, racing to the catalytic fulminations of the drum major, a red-bearded giant at least six-and-a-half feet tall, splendid in the full dress uniform of an Old Guard captain. His enormous bearskin shako marked time, forcing the musicians through their paces at an astonishing hundred beats per minute. They were absolutely running—a few steps forward, a slide to the side, an impromptu backward trot with a few intricate kicks mixed in—but not one braided cap, not one epaulet bobbled throughout the vast exercise, and when each rank trotted to the front, their belled coats jangled in unison.

The giant stiff-kicked the last hundred paces to the plane, shako bobbing, his huge beard forked to the heavens. His eyes were closed, his face bore the kind of cold rosy smile sculptors etch on the face of emperors. A few more kicks, a turn and then, still not missing a beat, he slammed his baton into the air, twirling it on elastic fingertips through a double figure-eight. His band—there were three hundred players if there was one—followed, executing the geometry with a precision that brought a dab of mist to Trout's eye.

Then he saw something that almost brought him to his feet. A dozen rows of women snaked to the rear of the band. Dressed in identical tri-color uniforms, their hair done up and capped by the revolutionary cockade, they sang, in the peak volume of trained lungs, the fervent lyrics of the French anthem. One hundred ladies to the row, this mass of matriarchal patriots raised a unitary throat to the song that sounded the first call to arms. In a series of absolutely matched, absolutely martial movements they measured out the noble yet humane intent of the *Marseillaise*, and their singing would have made even the grittiest of veterans weep.

He looked at them, gulped, and was stricken by their

sincerity, their robust, even bosomy voice. They were so close he could see them, the ample build and sturdy presence of Mediterranean women. Most were matrons, few were under twenty-five, and all were stout by any standards. The folds of their dresses, which fell daringly to mid-thigh, shook with each ponderous slap of leg to heavy leg. Their mouths, heaving and darkly lipsticked, ran as fast as the beat, perhaps several shades faster than the composer's original intent. At first Trout had trouble with the words. Then he realized that it wasn't French they were singing at all, but Maltese. He had never heard anything like it.

Certainly he never saw anything like what he was to see next. The chorus, like their band before, executed the same intricate double figure-eight as they approached the plane. Of course they added a few steps here and there as women will do, but they worked out the design in total concert, spreading in giant echelons into a single line that must have contained over a thousand strong.

Then they marked time while the band rolled to the right to address them, going through a maze of maneuvers that he could not follow, even if he had wanted to, for in that mile-long mark-time was revealed to his virginal vision that mighty chorus' posterior aspect. One thousand vigorous rumps, powdered and spangled in a wondrous outpouring of partisan symbolism that drew, magnified, and *locked* every iota of attention. Imagine two thousand plump thighs bouncing to the popping brass of the band up front, a white myriad wall of boots, swinging in fleshy counterpoint; a rolling sea of dimpled half-moons, surging to the fates; a bobbing bastion, risen above the plain; a sea of cold, fresh, hard rounds come from nowhere. He saw it, struggled harder to believe it with each jangling ounce of flesh, was caught in the curved cataclysm, pulled by the voluptuous excess into a perception of the thing's own esthetics. They could have walked on water and it wouldn't have caused him to raise an eyebrow. He had never seen such a ceremony, and without doubt would never see one again. But that it was infinitely right for its particular time and place, that it was a most *proper* celebration, of that Harry Trout was positive.

When they had wandered off and disappeared into the hushed distance, he looked at his watch calendar. The dial registered June 15, the precise anniversary of the day slightly more than a century earlier when Wellington and Napoleon had met for the first and last time. Waterloo!

It was only much, much later when the initial impact of that awesome Orphic force started to wear off, that Harry was restored to himself. Only then did he notice that the light had paled outside, and that it would soon be dusk. It was still another 1500 kilometers to Alexandria and he damn well didn't want to be up in the air over the Mediterranean at night, not in that rattletrap. Should he tell the Chief? Or maybe he had better hustle over to the flight tower and talk to the airport manager or whatever it was they called those chaps. Of course he didn't want to look insubordinate. Waverly was in command of the mission and it was clearly his responsibility to inquire as to its progress—but maybe the plane was unfit and they were being led by incompetents. He was wrestling with these rumblings when the pilot stumbled into the passenger space and seemed surprised to see him and the still-snoring Waverly fastened in their seats. After fumbling around for something plausible, the poor man finally let the cause of their delay unravel. It seemed that the airport director also played in the band's brass section. In his preoccupation with the band practice he had let his other duties slide—with awesome consequences. Flights were misdirected, civilian passengers were sent out on the wrong flights, and overall operations were in a shambles. A shipment of a thousand rare African violets destined for the London Botanical Gardens had been sent to Budapest, and theirs was the fifth incoming flight that day to be grounded. The airport had simply run out of fuel.

Things had gotten so sticky that the island's military governor roared up to the flight tower just before lunch hour and forcefully evicted the controller before his astonished staff. The airport was placed in the hands of the senior clerk who, being afraid to make any decisions, sent all incoming traffic on to Sicily. In the meantime the military governor thundered that he personally would see an end to the mess, and that relief was close at hand in the form of two destroyers that were at that moment loading aircraft fuel at Gibraltar for a fast dash to replenish the empty tanks at Malta. The expected arrival time of these Samaritans was set for 8:00 P.M. that forthcoming Thursday, two days hence. In the meantime the acting airport manager had invited his unwitting guests to enjoy the tent facilities the governor had so graciously established for them in an unused corner of the aerodrome—or to seek their own accommodations elsewhere on the island.

The pilot conveyed all of this woesome news to him in an admirably restrained manner, but there was no getting around it. They were in Malta for two days, not that he found that outpost disagreeable in the least. Of course, there were other compensations. He could do some rock-hunting, which he hadn't done since he'd been up in the Grampians. And he had witnessed a performance of the *Marseillaise* the likes of which few persons living or dead would ever see.

But he would have to wake Waverly and break the news to him. Almost wished he could let the man sleep.

Unlike the Calshot, the "Empress of Quebec's" trip was everything Mr. Lombardo had promised the 937 people to whom he had sold passage on her: smooth and uneventful. The figure was more precisely 936 for, although Professor Ambrose had sailed with the others, his tenure on the liner was but a precursor to a much rougher voyage. To the membership of the Lord Byron League, however, theirs was a journey into romance under soft tropical skies of the same hue and mood that, perforce, had inspired their young hero. They drew similar inspiration from the Mediterranean and, on the last night before debarking, delivered a spoken ode to Captain Crewes which, although featured as the evening's entertainment, ran considerably long. In all, forty separate poets gave voice to their creative triumph. These were counterpointed by a dozen perfervid choruses—mostly women—to give bulk to their delicate sopranos. The entire exegesis required somewhat better than three hours before its delivery. It was well past 11:00 P.M. when a full-throated burst of applause from the League's ranks signalled their approval of the work and, although most of the other passengers had long since gone to bed, Captain Crewes at least had struggled through wakefulness and was, even at that late hour, alert enough to record the event.

But the Lord Byrons were still not finished. At 10:00 A.M. the next morning, while the ship was disgorging net loads of luggage from each hold, and scores of stewards and sweaty longshoremen were climbing over the ramps and luggage piles trying to keep order, that muse-struck body emerged from the resplendent brass-and-glass doors of "A" deck's grand ballroom and, forming two lines, marched man and woman down the parallel ramps leading to the pier, which had been laid and rigged for the purpose. They wore long flowing robes of silk and gauze, the men in blue and the women in white— the poet's favorite colors—and the ladies had loosened their hair so that the sun was caught and focussed on a mass of greys and rinsed auburns. Twin maidens of thirty, more diaphanously clad than the others, raced down the ramps in front of their confreres, showering both rigging and astonished onlookers with handfuls of miniature tea roses. But by far the true highlight of the ship's arrival, and one which drew comment from Egyptian, British and Greek newspapers for months afterwards, was the stirring rendition of their hero's "Don Juan." The League spoke as one and moved as one, down the ramps and along the major boulevards of Alexandria in a dignified processional. They chanted as they went, first in English and then in Egyptian and the crowd, if they didn't grasp the poet's strophes, truly felt that "something marvellous was taking place," as the London *Times* was later to report.

The Biderbeck party got away as quickly as it could. The customs officer raised a few questions about the number of persons on their tally sheet, and Biderbeck had to exert some forceful language to bring the man into a more reasonable state. Captain Crewes' letter on the subject of the missing Professor Ambrose finally settled the matter, and they were allowed to leave the docks with three trucks loaded to the axle springs with the previously labelled contents.

Jonathan himself took the lead truck with Diana, still wearing one of her cruise outfits, making a very pretty driving companion. To show her spirit for adventure, she appeared at the parking area wearing a pair of skin-tight pigskin driving gloves, informing a much amused Biderbeck that she meant to do her share of the work. Arab drivers took the other two trucks, both six-tonners, half again as large as the first. Their route would take them straight down the Nile, through Cairo and the diggings at Fayyum to Amarna, a distance of 300 kilometers. They would meet Ted Stewart and Rosemont Baker in Amarna and then go on to their base camp, some five miles beyond the next bend of the river. Stewart was an old hand at the Biderbeck expeditions, having been recruited by Ambrose out of one of his tennis classes. He had been university trained, saw almost continuous service in the war, and worked off and on as a solicitor to keep a dry roof over his head. Stewart had no special talents as a digger, but was amiable and always seemed to know how to get a gauge unstuck, change a fuse, or cook up a good fondue.

Rosemont Baker, D. Sci., in contrast to the dilettante Stewart, was a short, squat bull of a man who was dead serious about his work. A Boer, born and raised in South Africa, Baker spent the first part of his life escorting wealthy English and American merchants on big game hunts. He had built it into a profitable profession, having acquired a double-verandahed house and a young, somewhat puffy blonde wife to go with it before he reached thirty. But a leopard had ended it all six months later when Baker got caught with a jammed magazine during a waterhole stakeout. The two hunters he was escorting managed to scare off the big cat with their elephant guns and the surgeons, after four operations, saved the leg— but in the process Baker lost his bank account, house, and fat blonde wife. Two years on the bum in Madagascar cleared his head of any sour thoughts about the whole business, but he couldn't work on the inside. If hunting was out he'd try medicine and go out in the bush after he finished school.

Baker was in the anatomy laboratory at Witwatersrand when they brought in the newly discovered skull of *Australopithecus*. From that day on Baker became an anthropologist, roaming about the quarries and dry lake beds of South Africa in search of fossil remnants of these earliest human antecedents. He was at Taungs when he met Biderbeck who, as usual, was travelling solo. The two men hit it off and Baker agreed to work with Biderbeck if something interesting came along. He was still digging at the limestone quarry a year later when he got a cable from that strange Englishman. The idea of digging in tombs struck his fancy. He signed on but wired Biderbeck that he would join the party at Amarna rather than waste time going to London. En route he met Ted Stewart at Nairobi, and got a more thorough rundown on Biderbeck.

Biderbeck was glad to have Baker around even though his talk was salty and he wore a brace of *howdah* pistols in his belt. Stewart could always be counted on to tighten morale. He had the other two men picked for their experience and given them the assignment of setting up the advance camp. Hackett was regular Army, having fought with Allenby. Shavers was a petroleum geologist by training and a swashbuckler by profession, having ranged over three continents wildcatting for oil. Both men were good workers, knew the desert as well as anyone else, and he had every confidence that the advance camp would be set up, watered and provisioned by the time they got there. He almost expected to meet old Ambrose there. Somehow the idea that the bulky professor had managed to make it back to London stuck in his mind, even though Crewes had insisted on being morbid about the affair.

While the Biderbeck party was gathering its forces for a final assault on Akhenaton's tomb, another caravan was moving toward that same objective, although minus the vast and complex technical accoutrements carried by the larger party. These had been installed years earlier deep within a natural cave network near the suspected burial vault. In its current transit of the sun-baked highway toward Amarna, the caravan consisted of a singularly dark vintage Rolls (ca 1915) whose rear windows, had one been able to see beneath the dust, evidenced a murky whiff of intrigue from their frosted and opalescent interiors. The Rolls, in turn, was followed by a calliope, jewelled, painted and festooned with the most intricate steel fittings, bright enough in all so that it would have been driven with pride in any circus van.

Both the car and calliope came from the "Empress of Quebec," having driven off unmolested in the highly charged ceremonies attending that vessel's docking. The driver had cared naught for Lord Byron nor his enraptured followers; he was in a hurry to be off. Only a fish seller witnessed their departure from the Alexandrian dock, noting a distinguished man cloaked in white direct his chauffeur, who definitely appeared to be a woman, while she linked the two vehicles with a leather-bound chain, watched while she ushered him into the back compartment, bowing politely as he entered. And watched with an ounce of muted wonder rising in his rasped chest as the strange caravan drove off with only the soft purr of an excellently tuned motor to mark its passing.

Anton Phibes was in a hurry, as much in a hurry as Biderbeck and yet, strangely enough, for a much more generous motive. They stopped for lunch at Fayyum—Phibes had admired the olive groves there as much as the mounds of pebbles that had once been pyramids—and then drove on, much refreshed by the repast of cold salmon and champagne.

They reached the site by mid-afternoon. Phibes had selected it for concealment as well as convenience. After negotiating the double switchback up a packed dirt spur road that surely looked like a dead end from the highway, he instructed Vulnavia to drive them into a rock-strewn box canyon which bore the weight of its ancient romance in lonely silence. For ten minutes they drove deeper into the walls, the sheer granite sides growing more jagged. Not a blade of grass relieved the parched rubble on the ground. More than anything it resembled the moon or some other dead planet where life, if it ever was, perished before the rocks themselves were born.

After one final long slow curve, in which the Rolls heaved and sighed with every yard of the dying, worn-out road, they reached their destination—a sheer granite wall whose bulk was already casting an early twilight on the grizzled floor.

Vulnavia pulled to a stop and Phibes, very eager now, got out and started toward the rock face. The litter was thicker underfoot and hard on his shoes, but wait! There was something else: tire tracks. Tire tracks, come and gone from nowhere, here in this place that he had counted on being private, that he had judged impregnable to any intruder. His eyes shot along the tracks' parallel angle, leading off from their own by about twenty degrees. They looked fresh but that was deceptive. Nothing wasted in the desert.

Well, there was nothing to be done about it. He had planned and prepared too long, and he would have to deal with any eventuality as it came.

He rummaged about the litter until he found that stone he had embedded years ago. He bent to pick it up, and had to exert some effort because the cable attached to its base led to the rock face. Another pull and a heavy granite slab swung forward on well-oiled hinges. The cave behind looked untouched, just as he had left it.

He signalled to Vulnavia and walked the last few yards into the entrance. Then he lit the torches, and watched as she guided the Rolls with the elaborate calliope in tow into a high-vaulted antechamber. Then, handing a torch to Vulnavia, they moved deeper into the maze through a series of narrow and oddly-cut corridors, and finally emerged into a broad aisle whose high walls were illuminated by a succession of paintings depicting Isis, Ptah and other minor gods.

Presently the paintings ended and the walls of the aisle broadened to form a long oblong hall. The wall at the other end was bare and solid. Phibes restored his torch to Vulnavia, felt along the wall on his right, inspecting each of its excellently crafted indicators until he located one burred and rougher than the others. He pressed it, gathering the accumulated delay of a long-wasted love's lifetime in his palm. He pressed the stone spot, after one hairline hesitation, to gather in the wasting, the loss, the long dry love, all of it, thinking everything and nothing of it. He pressed on, and they were in.

The stone apartment which was to be their home for the next brief period, opened with each new flash of a silk shaded lamp into a fresh aspect more intimate and tasteful than the one before. A rosewood china cabinet with bronze coatrack in the shape of a Nottingham elm, a bear-leather sofa, and endless shelves of books drew the apartment's outlines as ornate and comfortable as Phibes' Maldine Square mansion in London. The private quarters and the scientific laboratories and, of course, his special underground observatory were farther to the rear. His folio editions of John Dunne and John Skelton had been saved, as had his early E. A. Poe manuscripts. These were in their usual illuminated walnut display case. In its companion case rested Phibes' excellent collection of plate block covers.

He quickly surveyed these familiars, as befitted the master of the house. Actually very little had been lost in Maldine Square; the excursion had really been very simple. He had merely placed a prepaid order with Block and Sons, Movers, with instructions to move his complete furnishings by a certain date if they received no countermanding notice. He knew that it would require at least ten months for the authorities to establish tenure in the event they were obliged toward that course. The rest was simple. The Block people were to transship the shipment to a Marseilles warehouse where it would be met by a purchase order, made out under another name, and additional instructions.

At each turn in the rooms Phibes saw new evidence of the movers' thoroughness. Four mechanical members of Phibes Rag Time Wizards, the puppet orchestra he loved so much, sat staid and tuxedoed in their orchestra seats. They stared timelessly at the complete collection of the Phibes family lineage, each imposing portrait still in its gilt frame arranged on the wall opposite. Only his grandfather's likeness was missing but he imagined that whatever Orion Phibes was overseeing it would be the better for his staid presence.

Vulnavia was getting out the Sheffield service now. Time to celebrate their homecoming. His organ was over there somewhere under a drape. Ah, there it was, pink and healthy as ever. He swept off the dropcloth and sat down on the small plush seat. The keyboard spanned before him, beckoning in its intricacies. Yes, he'd have to play a celebratory note.

He turned on the switch, looked up at the stuffed eagle

suspended from a brass loop above, guarding the pipes, and cast a few tentative fingers on the keys. The pipes wheezed, showering sand on the parquet floor.

Vulnavia quickly attended to it, stepping into an adjoining room to empty her dustpan. When she returned, she was carrying a full-sized eagle as large as the first, only this one was alive, his claws gripped firmly to her glove.

Phibes nodded at his pet and resumed his playing, this time the notes coming out clean.

Abruptly a tune took form, gathered, and filled the rock-bound apartments with a racy, almost awkward rhythm. It was a new number that Phibes had heard on the cruise: "The Sheik of Araby."

He bent to it, pedalling and riffling into a hard beat. Vulnavia turned the lights down low. It was good to be back; very, very good to be back.

Chapter 7

"Sonsabitchin' flies'll eat the sonsabitchin' hat off yer bloody head before you can get yer sonsabitchin' hand up to swat 'em. Ya ruddy beetle-assed bugger, come back here!" Hackett slammed his helmet into the sand and stomped after the black speck. Even though it was after four it was still so damn hot that Shavers couldn't blame his partner for popping off. The older man's big belly lurched and swung over his thick legs as he bounded over the rubble, kicking up big puffs of dust with his hot boots. The fly could have gotten away if he had been a caterpillar, because Hackett got his sweat up right away, and after three or four hops his face was so wet he kept blinking his eyes to get rid of the damp.

"You better cut that out, big man, he's got the drop on you." Shavers ran the stake bed right across Hackett's path, and swung back around at him.

"Hey, mate, you back? What'd you find out there today?" Hackett flopped against the side of the truck, then bounced right off again. "Sonsabitches! that's hot!"

"Today I found something different, a lot of sand. Wouldn't be surprised there's enough for a desert."

"You goin' to call it a day? Because if you are, that's two of us." Hackett had his red handkerchief out of his shorts and was blotting his face.

"Better not, Hackett. If the others from Nairobi met Biderbeck on schedule, the whole bloomin' lot'll be out here day after tomorrow. Knowing Mr. Biderbeck, I'd like to have finished what we're supposed to survey. Goin' to fill up my canteen and have one more run around them hills."

"Sure you didn't find an oasis with some dancing girls, you old billy goat?"

"No, but I'll keep it in mind. Right now I'd even settle for a bloomin' mirage!" Shavers finished filling his canteen, swung the truck around and zipped back out across the dunes. He was gone in less than half a minute and the place got quiet again. Hackett almost wished that fly would come back. The spot they had picked couldn't have been more isolated. It wasn't really the Nile valley but the edge of the Sahara, so that everything west of them for about a thousand miles was sand dunes. To the east rose a string of rock ridges with Amarna somewhere on the other side. Between the rocks and the sand they had exactly one palm tree, a deep well that worked only in fits, and a deadline to meet. Hackett dragged the big tent out of the truck. If he got the thing up that afternoon he could work on the surveying with Shavers in the morning, which beat lugging a 300-pound sack of canvas around at that time of day.

While Hackett banged away at the tent pegs, his partner was moving across the dunes at full throttle. Shavers had been a platoon leader during the war where he made a name for himself as a marauder. His specialty was the short devastating raid, where surprise and firepower settled the business quickly. He worked with three or four small trucks and mounted four 50-caliber machine guns on them, plus a mortar squad in each. Waterholes and supply caravans were the usual targets. He'd make two passes, sending his gun

trucks right through the enemy at forty miles an hour, crisscrossing so that the guns could do their work on both sides. The mortars finished off whatever was left. After the war they gave him the D.S.O. and asked him to
stay on and take a commission. He tried it for a year but the forms and reports got the best of him. He resigned, put his severance pay into surveying equipment, and had been on the move ever since.

This was his second time back in Egypt since the war. He had worked for Biderbeck that first time too, in Fayyum. The man was a stickler but he paid top dollar. He didn't much care for grave-digging, but Biderbeck was the kind of man who didn't talk too much about what he was after; he said what he wanted, and then counted on its being done. This little jaunt actually was a drop from the blue, since his money was short and, with the combines taking over, things were tight in Texas.

Well, he'd give the man what he wanted. He had one more bench mark to check, then he could go back, split a couple cans of beer with Hackett and sack out. He wanted to get an early start in the morning so they could have the road laid out on schedule.

Shavers found the mark after poking around the canyon an extra half-hour. He put a cairn around it so it would be easier to spot. He had thrown his shovels into the truck and was backing out when he heard music—organ music! He let the motor idle for a minute but it kept coming. It sounded like it was coming right out of that rock face up front.

He drove right up to the end of the canyon but the damn music got louder. It was like a total mirage: no lakes or dancing girls, just this crazy organ banging away in the middle of a decrepit burial ground. And it wasn't even church music, but something right out of a dance hall. He turned the motor off but the thing just kept coming.

He had better take a look. Biderbeck didn't like mysteries.

He got past the first Crosshatch of tunnels by following the sound. It boomed in a straight line—big and hollow as a heavy drill. The tunnel sides shook, trickles of dust streamed down, and the floor jumped with the drones. He saw the pictures, a bunch of ancient scrolls. He felt like a midget crawling into an enormous radio. If he had ever seen a ghost this would have been the time, but Shavers was a practical man and this was some bastard's idea of a joke. Probably a wireless hooked up to an amplifier stuck deep in the mountain. The bloke must have found out something about Biderbeck's plans that no one else knew and was trying to scare him off. The Egyptian used a lot of gold in their tombs. That must be it, or jewels. He had seen pictures of the funny headwear, all gold and pearls; snake amulets with ruby eyes; cats with diamond brooches and gold teeth, and long, mean crocodiles flaked in emeralds.

Biderbeck had set things up so that everyone would get a percentage. After the big boodle at King Tut's tomb, the stakes got pretty high out in the desert. He heard a lot of talk about it back in Texas. Some people tried to sign up, even planned to organize combos to go after the tombs, like they did for oil. Rock drills, blasting powder, the works – except no one knew much about Egypt. And then there was fear of catching a disease from the mummies – bubonic plague or typhus or something almost as deadly. So it was mostly talk.

But Biderbeck was the kind of slick customer who could pull it off. Tight as a clam with people on the outside, but pretty straight otherwise. And he had his licences. Probably told the authorities he was going to take photographs. He was a cool one, all right.

The music was so loud that Shavers covered his ears. When he saw the lights he knew there was some kind of plot underway. No one was supposed to be around these hills but Biderbeck's crew, and he was sure they wouldn't be groping around inside the cave without settling at camp first. Besides, they were off the track. The old map located Akhenaton's tomb a few points to the north. Of course you never could tell; the army was more interested in wells than dead kings. Either that, or this was someone else's grave. It sure had enough pictures spread sround. And if it *was*, he had first claim on it. He'd have to tell Biderbeck, but the biggest percentage was his in a case like this.

He was running now, very excited about his fabulous find. A few more turns—the music was enough to crack the mountainside—and he saw the rooms. An apartment of some kind all lit up by soft lamps, furniture and rugs spread around. Hokie Jamokies! It looked like people were living in it. There *were* people in it, a bunch of musicians. No, they were dummies; the music was coming from another room.

He edged in through a hallway and saw them. A chap in a white cloak was at the organ, a big pink glass machine, banging away. And a girl; She could be his daughter.

"Hey!"

The girl was looking. There! She spotted him, was looking at him. She was coming toward him looking mad, crazy mad, sort of.

"Hey!"

Now the man saw him, too. He didn't look mad, just a bit unhappy. The guy was nodding at the girl. Then he hit the keys. Doomsday itself struck! He had better get some help. Better get back to Hackett.

He took another look. The girl was letting something go. Holy Lord, it looked like a hawk, but bigger! An eagle!

He swung the light down and ran straight back along the larger corridor, hoofing it to get away. Now he heard the wings, like an angel's breath behind him in the dark. He started zigzagging and swung the light up for another look. He couldn't see it—just the sighing of those wings over that crazy organ.

He rounded the wall's edge and started groping into the maze. He felt something crush his shoulder, then an awful sharp, hard lurch, enough to tear his jacket.

He ran faster, swinging the light up every other step to keep the thing away. Then he caught a glimpse of a blur in front of him. The eagle! Its wings must have been ten feet across.

He was ducking now but be could hear it passing over his head. The goddam thing was coming quicker, making short dives with its feet straight down. He couldn't let it get near! He held up his arms and swung hard.

Augh! The claws raked his arm to the elbow like a string of hard razors pulled against the bones. He felt the blood drop to his face; he lowered his arm but kept trying to zig-zag. Had to get out to the truck. Like a fool he had left his gun back there. If he'd only taken it, he'd blow the bloody bird's head off.

A knife, then another caught his shoulder. The thing was on him. Heavier than he thought. Get rid of it. Get rid of it before it knocked him down. The wings were all over him now, and the beak. It was on his shoulder, neck, hand. His ear tore. He could feel it tear. He was going down if he didn't get rid of it. Maybe . . .

He twisted free, spinning with his one good side and bounced into the wall, blotting it with a great swatch of blood.

It was harder to run now. Breathing was short. Must be

getting weaker. His head was hot, burning. He felt his head where his ear should have been. It was gone!!

He lurched on but could hear the damn thing coming again. He ran, lurched, poked, invested the last shreds of his strength, and could see some light far up ahead. He started to run for it. He had to make it.

His legs were moving but the thing was closer. A sweep. And another. And then it closed. A million needles. A knife. A sharp iron knife. Shades. The feather shades closing. The eagle was on his back. It would have been so simple to shoot. But his arms—the claws had severed his back muscles and his arms were gone. He was dropping, falling, dropping down, but it stayed with him. In blind effort he still ran, swinging his legs in the dust even though he was down, even though the blood from his scalp flooded his eyes and his hands wouldn't raise to clear them. He would have, could have moved himself. Get out first and get the gun. That was a good thought, enough to carry him through. Also his last thought, as the great bird closed over him and put his beak deep, very deep into his throat.

Biderbeck got to the camp a day early. He was the kind of a man that could be prompt and prissy when he was early, a condescending ramrod when he was late. Either way, time seemed to be the natural enemy of Mr. Biderbeck. He revelled in and despised clocks, and was known to throw watches to the pavement when their mechanisms miskept the hour. He loathed schedules yet he lived by them. In transit he pawed over timetables, only to be constantly late for meals en route. In traffic he scourged cab drivers to get him to appointments on time. Once there, he would promptly walk a block or two to take some air.

As much as he was obsessed by time, he was more

addicted to detail. His personal habits were without fault Suits went to the cleaners once a month and were hung in his closet with the open side of the hanger facing out. Yogurt and preserves, preferably gooseberry or blueberry, constituted his breakfast, which he took with black Jamaican coffee. He exercised each day for twenty minutes and squeezed hard rubber handballs to strengthen his wrists. He kept his personal articles inventoried, installed labels on his furnishings, and knew where everything could be found. His meals were planned six months in advance; he bought provisions, with the exception of fresh vegetables and fruits, once a year in November. He wisely spent one week in hospital for an annual checkup and insisted that Diana keep to a similar watchfulness after she came to live with him. When he took spirits it was in large quantities, but with no apparent loss of facility. At home Biderbeck consumed champagne at breakfast, cold American beer for lunch and unblended scotch two ounces at a time in the evening. At social functions he was somewhat more forceful. Arming himself with an eight-ounce tumbler filled to the brim with whiskey, he displayed a progressive brilliance of speech that made Jonathan Biderbeck a prize acquisition amongst hosts with social pretentions. Of course his gorgeous Diana had to be given some of the credit. Poise, bearing, looks, intelligence, gentleness of heart—the young girl had everything, and with Biderbeck's wealth her stock was awfully high indeed amongst the younger bachelors. Some, especially those who couldn't perceive her position vis a vis Biderbeck, tried to impress their devotion upon her on occasion, but Diana's tact in handling these sorties was as efficient as it was painless. Once it didn't work, however, and an aroused Biderbeck was forced to shove the chap through a French window for his troubles.

The whole lot descended on Philo Hackett just as he was finishing his lunch coffee, and he was damned glad he'd busted his gut the night before getting the tent up. The water drums, all but one, were full, so that wasn't too bad. That damned Shavers was out somewhere on the road, probably hunting one of those bloody surveying marks and got caught in the dark. Shavers should have known better than to get stuck like that. If he stayed away much longer he'd have trouble explaining things to Biderbeck.

Biderbeck seemed pleased enough with the advance camp but had been too wrapped up with the unloading business to talk much about anything else. He was pretty damn jumpy about the packing cases and kept chewing out the Arabs something awful whenever they got sloppy.

"*Swachan moolji baswa, Baswa!*" The turbanned man was a head taller than Biderbeck but he scurried out of the tent flap under the sharp words.

"I see no reason why we can't begin my schedule promptly at eight tomorrow. You know yourself that time is of the essence, if my deductions are correct." Biderbeck switched talk so quickly Hackett blinked.

"It's just Shavers. *Always* made it a point to get back an hour before sunset, sir. I think the first order of business is to send someone. . . ." Hackett decided that was the best approach. Just lay it out straight and let the man work with it. If Biderbeck was that damn tied up with details he'd think first about losing his geologist.

"You and Shavers are two of my best men, Hackett. That's why I trusted you both out here before the main party. He can take care of himself. I'm not worried."

Biderbeck's brisk answer surprised Hackett. The man wasn't new to the desert. He should have known better. He started to get angry but decided against it. He kicked the floor instead. "Frankly, I'm worried, sir. I don't know where the hell he got to last night. Said he had to check his markers. All he had with him was the junk in the truck, and two canteens aren't enough for two days. Not up in these hills, they ain't."

"You've been reading too many newspapers, Hackett. Ever since that Tut-Ahkh-Amon business a new curse turns up each week. Just as well, I say. Every damn fool and his brother would be out here with picks and shovels. It would be worse than a gold rush."

"Maybe so, sir, but I think we ought to have a look. And don't get me wrong; I'm not trying to sound gloomy. It's just that the more you live in the desert, the more ways you find you can *die* in the desert."

Just as Biderbeck started to chew on that Stewart and Baker came in, each carrying an armload of rifles and looking more like hunters than dedicated archaeologists. He showed them the gun locker, then called everyone together, including Diana, who had been unpacking her personal luggage in one of the tent's smaller compartments.

"Ah, are we all here now? Well then, my first and only 'formal' speech. Tomorrow all of us will begin what I know will be the most satisfying work of our lives. I know we shall succeed, succeed beyond your wildest imagination. Let me show you what we're going to be doing, and we'll go out for a quick reconnoiter before nightfall."

On a signal the Arabs removed a tarpaulin from the model of Akhenaton's tomb. Biderbeck peered at the others, a flush of triumph in his expression. As usual, he had surprised them. By waiting until the last possible moment to put all his plans together he added the necessary edge of excitement. He had told them much earlier that they were going to look for a Pharaoh's tomb, and he had also given them some background about the Heretic King and the fabulous city he had built up at Amarna. But rumors about treasures were old hat, and anyone who knew anything about Egyptian history knew that for every successfully sealed royal tomb there were twice as many successful grave robbers.

The model's real impact was in its detail. It had been carefully constructed from Pi Ankhi's description. The Chief Servitor's comments had been included in the segment of the Osiris papyrus found at Thebes, in a vault whose seals were still intact upon discovery. If they were truly unbroken, then the odds were almost perfect that Akhenaton's tomb had remained closed to all intruders: *almost* perfect.

At that same moment another element of Pi Ankbi's most excellent puzzle was under careful watch. Illustriously dialed by intricate scrollwork of mother of pearl, its obsidian face polished to mirror brilliance, this moon clock appeared to be what it actually was: a machine of ancient and wondrous design that could plot the course of the important heavenly bodies for a thousand generations. It had been widely used by the astronomers of the Empire— as well as during more tranquil periods of Egyptian life— in charting the movements of the sun and moon and predicting their extra-terrestrial influence upon the Nile's flow. Plans for this particular model had been duly noted by Pi Ankhi. His notes were on the segment of the Osiris papyrus lost during the sack of Constantinople. Antiquarians were uniform in their agreement that it would be impossible to know what was on that segment without actually seeing it, but speculation was rife that a penultimate step to the discovery of Akenaton's tomb was sequestered with the missing fragment. Of course, all attempts at tracking down that elusive portion after Constantinople's fall met with failure.

But Anton Phibes was a resourceful man, and a patient man. Close to his goal and pleased with the course of circumstances, he studied the moon clock's Roman numerals as they slowly slid from "8" to "7."

Vulnavia, after the minor intrusion of a day earlier, busied herself with the apartment's furnishings. In keeping with the external surroundings Phibes had requested that all interior decorations be similarly ancient, preferably from the Eighteenth Dynasty, which contained the tenure of Akhenaton's reign. She had just arranged the last of a group of animal amulets on a shelf when she noticed that her mentor was attempting to talk to her. Hoping to forestall his embarrassment, she plugged in his throat jack before he could notice the oversight.

"I am now convinced that the modern world has no knowledge of this great complex of tombs, because the ancient Egyptians divided the Nile into many underground channels to flood them." Phibes strolled about the wall where she had already hung some faded but still rather concise panels. "But if my calculations are correct, once in every five hundred years, when the moon and sun are in proper conjunction, the waters will drop and flow back into the magical River of Life, at the end of which lies the last supply of this elixir which has the power to restore life—and to maintain it!"

Phibes' voice rose at that. He stood before the drawing of the precious vial like a man possessed. Now there could be no doubt about his purpose.

When Victoria died, Anton Phibes had taken two vows: the first, to execute her killers; the second, to restore her own life. Phibes was a learned man, a man who could not be thought of as violent. Certainly one could not imagine a man of his taste and temperament going about the business of murder. He was also a trained and competent scientist in disciplines where potions and elixirs had long since gone out of fashion. The first of his vows had been fulfilled with a verve and compression unequalled in many acts of recorded murder, and by his current excitement it looked as if his second now would bear a similar result.

"Seven more days remain to find the tomb of Akhenaton, and with it, the key. We must be there this year, this week, to be carried on the bosom of the River of Life."

He was overcome with emotion at the thought. He pulled the jack from his throat and staggered onto a lounge. Vulnavia was at his side immediately, emptying a glass of port into his parched neck aperture. His eyes remained closed. To help him rest, she placed a recording of his famed "Elegy to the Element" on the Victrola. Then she sat in the chair opposite, watchful, as always, of her master in repose and relaxation. His own voice was Phibes' best inspiration.

"One is a casque to the infinity of motions that burned in the gloved hands of the gods, this world becomes . . ."

On signal the musicians raised their instruments and began to play the accompanying lyrics, composed by Phibes himself. His voice held firm, a strong, earthy recitation of the poet's timber.

> "Fierce we are sundered and tried,
> Joined, time taken, time revived.
> A third time's tortured torment
> Of this meeting, renewed in
> Commonplace brass and glass,
> Shall in connection lie because the sun
> Moon, planets, stars, all
> Roaring bodies be, and be
> This lined night as one.
> "If death from life depends

On the callowed strain of blood
To bone, ourselves pressed to
Plaintive wedges, shadows of
Private selves, cast to counterfeit,
Then we as much can count
That life from death becomes
'Ere these globes run us all
On heaven's course, on heaven's
Long night course."

Phibes lifted his eyes at the last pourings of his voice. The "Elegy," written when he was but a youth, always tamed him whether stabbed by love, the cold thought of death, or run through by the arrogant grasp of fates. The past beckoned and he would have liked to sleep, to feel the sweet relaxation of bones that his old words brought. But time had gone. He had no more of it.

He beckoned to Vulnavia. Her face flamed. She came. She would have kissed him. He noticed that in her of late. She tried to get close to him and press his face, hands, skin. In years past he would have resented it, but it mattered less now. She was good. She allayed him. She did what he wanted.

They went into the tunnels, this time deeper into the mountain on the other side of the apartment. Vulnavia held two torches and it was good that she did, for it was a grim region stinking of death.

They came to a "V" and went to the left—into a blank wall. Tracked back again and over onto the other side. Another "V," another long corridor, then doubled back. They were in a cross-hatch.

Phibes checked his maps, made a smudge on the wall and went on. They went ten paces without seeing it; twenty paces; twenty-five. They were out

Paintings lined the walls now. Cheap scribblings, tortured in an odd way. The drawings of the workmen before they died. The walls were convex, narrowed. They were in a chute, a smaller and smaller space into black. He found a loose stone and stepped on it. The drawing with three ibexes parted slightly. Phibes pressed with his foot.

They stooped and were in a very large corridor, dripping wet. The walls and ceiling were still wet. The floor had little rivulets in its creases. Then came the bones: fragments of a leg and hand; ribs in place but some of them shattered. Then one intact, stretched, spear in hand as if he was running, and another with a shield. Farther on a lower frame were animal bones, heavy jawbone, sharp teeth, claws—a lion. The workers' death warrant; at least they'd been given spears.

Then they heard the water above their heads, rushing, churning fast, but not on their level. It was up above; a few more steps and it was gone.

But was it? Ahead was a pool on the floor they had to splash through. Then on up a ramp, a long, dark ramp.

The paintings had stopped. There was no water. The creases in the stone were smaller. No signs of life. Nothing.

A few more steps up. Then Phibes was pawing. One.,. Two . . . Three . . . He felt, reached, had it. He took a small mallet from his cloak, tapped a bit more. The block of stone edged back and continued to edge back, cracking open the seal of centuries.

Phibes bent to the wall now and pushed—pushed with all the strength of his anguish. He pushed with the total perception of what he lost; of what he stood to gain. His back, legs, head arched, slanted, strained backward—and the block moved; moved again, and opened. And they were in.

It is said that Queen Nefertiti conceived a permanent and celestial vision on the night before she was wed. Her dream described the royal couple's happiness and works on earth and made a prediction of its manifold rewards in their next life together. Her vision also contained a prophecy, spoken by the great Aton, that Nefertiti and her king would realign the fates of the earth and all its people when they lived in the other world. But they would have to marry again in death, as in life.

So convinced was the gorgeous queen of the Aton's intention that she appealed and won from Akhenaton the right to design their second nuptial chamber. During their marriage she devoted the breadth of her soul and the poetry of her heart to this task. She continued her devotions even when the royal household was beset with enemies during Amarna's last years. And at the end, exiled and separated from her king, she prevailed. The result of Queen Nefertiti's labors now greeted Anton Phibes, and to his tired eye and heart, wearied of a love too long lost, the shimmering exaltation of that chamber's aspect restored one small measure of hope.

A long golden snake graced the central sarcophagus. Phibes moved forward. He raised his hand to touch it.

A shot, and another and several more cracking the stone air.

A shot meant people. Outside! Close by!!

Stones fit to stones. Passages shut in flight. Heels pattering against the quartered light. Phibes retreated and retraced his steps. The thought of intruders was abominable. He could *feel* them, could hear them again talking, harsh voice full of purpose.

". . . this entry has long been recognized as the principal entrance to the Mountain of the Dead. Look, Diana, these bones are those of the workmen who sealed up the various tombs and who were killed so they could never reveal how to reach them..."

It was Biderbeck! The girl was trembling. An asp, its head sliced clean, lay nearby.

"I'm not superstitious but somehow I feel we're trespassing; that we shouldn't be here." Biderbeck put his arm around the girl. She murmured into his shoulder. Another man, in white jodhpurs and a leopard bush hat, watched. He seemed relieved when Biderbeck pulled away.

"I believe that this entry has been deliberately described for ages as the only way into this mountain, and that there are several hidden passageways which may not originate here at all. Tomorrow we'll each take a different area and look thoroughly into every nook and cranny. We'll bring all the heavy equipment..."

So that was it! They were going to tear the mountain apart. Pillage it. Ruin it. Perhaps take what was his. In that single minute Anton Phibes made his death decision. These people, led by the man Biderbeck, were bent on preventing him from keeping his second vow. His efforts, at first to discourage them, and then to send them off, had failed. They would have to die. When he moved back into the mountain he was already making plans. He would work long and late that night.

Ted Stewart also stayed up late that night. Being a persistent bachelor had its minor triumphs as well as its major inconveniences. The late evening shave was one of those comforts. When he was in town he changed for supper and then again if he was going out. If he had an "important" evening with a new girl he used his straightedge razor and took special care. He felt that was a sure way to avoid the major inconvenience that was the affliction of his single estate: sharing his bed with none but the pillows.

When he was in school married life was looked upon as the anvil around a decent man's neck: a demanding wife, squealing brats, and a flat filled with furniture still on contract. Compared to that a bachelor was a king. He could go and come as he wanted, work only when the need arose, enjoy the newest cars, the latest clothes and the best restaurants. Best of all he could have his pick of the ladies, a new one every year—even every month if that's the way he wanted it.

But the picture didn't quite fit the facts. Oh, being a solicitor was all right. He got his share of "good" cases, and made just enough to pay the rent on his four newish rooms near Grosvenor Square and keep the car payments up on the best last year's model he could find. He had eight suits, the extra one being for special events; six pairs of shoes, all hand-lasted; And enough shirts, ties and hats to turn out in a new combination every day in the month.

He could afford to dine out more often than he did. But he outfitted his kitchen with an eye toward the practical— he wanted to "entertain" at home—so he developed a good way with the chafing dish and the roasting pan.

But the ladies Ted Stewart met fell into two large categories: matrons and "working girls." The former he had tested and found wanting. The few short-lived affairs he had had with his married clients left him with the intelligence that modern feminine frigidity is best left alone. The working girls on the other hand—the secretaries, seamstresses, nurses and other women of marriageable age that Ted Stewart did meet—were, almost uniformly, chill, inert, yes, even repelling. And if they were not then they were expensive.

The result was that after twelve years of bachelor life Ted Stewart, far from achieving the life of a smooth, well-turned-out bedroom acrobat, found that many of his nights each month were spent alone—far too many nights.

He was alone this night. After supper he had shaved and changed his linen. He tried playing hearts with Baker, but the man's conversation put him off. A nip of cognac didn't help either. In short, he was restless. To make matters worse, he had caught a glimpse in the main tent after Biderbeck and Diana had turned in; the light was still on and he could see the clear silhouettes. They hadn't even waited until they got to bed. It drove him wild. Mercifully, Diana reached over the table or whatever it was she was holding onto, and turned out the lamp.

After that Stewart did the only thing he could think of to help his condition: he took a walk. At least the desert air was cold, and he might get tired enough to get to sleep later.

He hadn't been walking twenty minutes when he saw it He had to slap his head. With the way his mind was running it took a couple of slaps to believe it, but there she was.

She was swaying slightly. Her veils were lofted by the night air; her legs trilled with bells.

He walked closer, slapping his head again. The *houri* didn't go away. She moved a little faster, her legs switching in the veils. Then she beckoned.

He followed.

She walked on, her movements undulant to the sand.

He got closer—just the two of them under the black sky.

She reached the crest of a dune and beckoned again.

He gained the top in a second. And there beheld the infinitude of pleasures poeticized by Omar Khayyam. A tent of the purest white silk was spread in the depression before him, held firm and upright by poles of ivory topped by gold.

Music drifted from within its perfumed folds, promising everything else within. She entered, swaying, raising her hand again.

He followed, passed a few coppers of *backsheesh* to the old Bedouin at the tent flap, and went in.

It was all there: silk pillows, musicians in burnooses reeling out a tune on their reeds and cymbals; trays of meat, wines, nuts; and the girl, with her outer veils removed; absolutely diaphanous.

She beckoned to the chair of honor and he sat in it, a great gold frame in the form of a scorpion.

Then the musicians struck an upbeat. She began with one hand meeting, stroking, stretching, starting the other parts of her. Her feet moved in counter rhythms, faster than the breath of devils. She turned, doubled, was grace, flesh, a wailing bank of jelly.

The music moved faster.

Veils were shedding, skin was opening. Her mouth opened, her eyelids lifted, opened. Her legs . . .

The music swelled, slowed, swelled. She was on him now, above him, the scent and sense of her armpits dazzling his own. She slid to him, to the sides of him, above him. Her croft captured him once; her knobs a second time; her lips a third. She was gone.

But not yet.

Behind him now was a sea of motion pressing his back, his neck, his ears. He had to have her. Reached up. Couldn't.

He couldn't touch her, couldn't move his arms.

The music stopped.

She stopped.

The Bedouin entered, removed a key, and then his hands were locked to the chair.

He looked at the man, but he was gone in an instant.

He looked again. He wanted to see her and she reappeared, this time with a small jar. She put the key inside, placed it a few paces from the chair, and was gone.

Minutes later he heard them outside moving about. And as quickly, the tent, pillows, musicians, trays, foods—everything was gone.

He remained.

He was alone under the dark night sky. A damned joke. Some damned joke!

He'd have to get that key before he froze. He shoved his feet.

The chair didn't move.

He shoved again.

Nothing.

Again. And again. Very hard now. The chair edged forward.

Again.

Another few inches.

And again, and again, until he had it. The jar. He had it with his feet, picked it up, dropped it

Nothing.

He pushed the jar up again and dropped it again.

It broke. The key fell out, and something else—a lot of something else.

Scorpions.

He was dead.

Chapter 8

He was moving closer to her now. She could feel the mass of wool blankets pulling on her shoulders. Her back tingled and her hair was all over the pillow. She wanted to look outside but her eyes felt awfully good closed like that. And it was cold, very cold when she got to sleep. She would just stay that way for awhile.

It was so good just to stretch out under the bedding. Getting unpacked was work. They were really in the desert: red sand and rock. You had to compensate when you walked, and the sun baked the energy out of you.

She was a little frightened when Jonathan first told her she could come. But she had gotten through the first day all right. She even enjoyed organizing things, watching the bare sand turn into a cluster of tents, a place to live in that immense landscape. By nightfall she was bone-tired and glad to have Jonathan alone.

He was closer now. His legs touched hers. Her back was unwinding, softly unwinding in his hands. Her peignoir was bunched up around the small of her back. She would have to undo it if he was going to do her there and her neck as well. That was the best, when he stroked her neck. She tried to get at the silk cords, but they were under her. She shifted and felt him move in closer.

She slid the knot open and with a lazy eye looked out from under the pillows. It was dawn, or close to it. She ducked back under as his hand reached to her neck. He was molding her now, turning, petting, shaping at both ends of her back, smoothing her tired skin.

Then she felt it, a creamy layer of soft heat. He had put oil in his palms, rippling them in every hollow of her back, squeezing her shoulders, neck and bottom into a new waiting. She was oiled, oily now. The warmth was in her, going with his hands. Her nipples felt it, condensed, stood out. She shifted her leg, sliding it against the other to let his hand in. But he waited, took it slow, keeping his hand working in the small of her back. Working in deep and strong, his fingers courted her skin, tracing a circle, then larger circles; shaping her bottom, rounding out its sides, their round, crisp edges, circling deeper and lower, tracing the tops of her thighs.

She moved, wanted to push her belly into the cot, wanted to stretch, grab the pillow with her hands, wanted to ease the palpitations — she almost laughed at that word — in her chest. She wanted to soften her nipples so they wouldn't sting; she wanted his hands.

He was in her hard, hard on her now.

He got up above and came down hard. Kicking her knees out to the sides he came down and was coming down again, staying in her while he moved for a third. She rolled further over on her belly, tried to edge her legs apart to help him, but he moved faster, pressing her firmly into the sheets.

She smiled, thought about how good it was last night, and drifted off.

He was still over her when the alarm rang. She must have been drowsing for a half-hour. Some pillows were under her and he held her around the middle. His head was close to hers, breathing as hard as she was. She wanted to bite him, reached back, but grabbed the edge of the cot instead. The damn alarm was still ringing. She wanted to stop it but she couldn't possibly do anything now. His pressure was all over her back, sides, and bottom, concentrating, concentrating with every push.

The alarm was ringing. She opened. He started. She opened more, and felt the heat pressing. He pressed and was pressing. They were starting. The heat was heavier now, and more. Pressing. The alarm.

They were there.

Jonathan Biderbeck was the best lover in the world and she would be his protégé, mistress, wife, or any which way he wanted it. Diana Trowbridge finished the last touches of her make-up, adjusted her scarf, and got ready to greet the second day of her great adventure. With a man like Biderbeck she could have gone to the moon, tacked after sharks in the Indian Ocean, set out for the North Pole, or even stayed in this desert digging for a dozen kings from a dozen dynasties. He was one gorgeous man. Everything she had met at school or on the reception line paled in comparison. She was beginning not to give one good damn who noticed her affection for him. She opened her jewel case, took out the pearl bracelet, then replaced it for the opals. If she was going to be treated like a queen, she certainly intended to look like one.

While Diana was thus starting her day preparatory to gracing the now fully organized camp, two official travellers were bearing down upon that outpost with a haste and determination that underscored the importance of their mission—and if Detective Trout and Division Chief Waverly had begun their morning less sweetly than Miss

Trowbridge, their accomplishments by that early hour were far more portentous.

Waverly, for all his bluster, possessed one singular operating philosophy: that of protecting British subjects. Irascible, bombastic rooster that he was, Wembley Waverly took his duties seriously. True, he loathed crime and criminals and wanted to catch them wherever he could, but he much preferred protecting his charges before crimes happened to them than attending to their travails afterward.

It was precisely for that reason that Waverly delayed their already much-delayed excursion by calling at the British Embassy in Cairo. This time it was Trout who insisted that they keep moving. After his year-long malaise and retreat, his blood was up. All the signs, clues and surroundings pointed to his old nemesis. Where even the whisper of the name Phibes would have jolted Harry Trout's high speed faculties, the advent of Adam Ambrose on his beach at Margate told him above all else that it was showdown time.

The air trip had been merely tolerable. Malta, where the only worthwhile cave was guarded by a herd of goats, proved to be a two-day nightmare. His chief's insistence that they detour to Cairo almost had him shouting at Waverly. He wanted to catch Phibes! A visit to the British Embassy, when that fiend was running about the pyramids, was not the way to get on with the pursuit.

But visit the Embassy they did, and after two hours of haggling with insubordinates, Waverly came away with what he was after, but only after carrying the matter to the Ambassador himself. The objective of his persistence— an order revoking Biderbeck's licenses—Waverly could have had sooner, but for his official host's indisposition. A succession of fêtes earlier in the week had brought the man to terms with his gout. Waverly had to talk over the bandages to win his case, but he could be boundlessly eloquent when the safety of the Empire or her subjects was challenged. That he did not understand the peril was proven soon enough.

Waverly bought two orange squashes which at least got them off to a decent start. Then he stopped at El Gizeh for late breakfast, but all they could find was some lamb fried with cashews and a disgusting honey-barley porridge. Trout wanted to skip it, but he was afraid of pressing Waverly too hard.

They drove on. It got hotter, if such could be imagined, and Trout's belly bubbled like a still. The government truck jolted and wrenched his ribs. The sand pitched more than the open seas. The pressures in his lower organs multiplied past all danger points. With each agonizing yard he felt worse, and worse again. He wanted to ask Waverly to stop the truck, but luck was running with him now. The Division Chief pulled off just in time. The seats were too hot and the dashboard radiated like an oven. They had to get the canopy overhead.

Trout rummaged around in the luggage compartment but the damn thing was gone. He poked around under the seats and turned up some cloth. When they spread it out it looked like a flag of sorts—green stripes on yellow with some Arabic writing along the edge. Probably from the military, but it was better than nothing. They rigged it up with some coat hangers and were back on the road in a few minutes, continuing their mission under a mysterious standard, its green tassels bravely bounding. Trout had the wheel. Waverly was staring stolidly at the landscape. He had lost the pink glazed look of his earlier indignation and his skin was glowing slightly now.

"Bloody few landmarks hereabouts. Never fails. No landmarks, no civilization."

"I say sir, there's something now. What's the map say about that?"

Waverly shuffled some papers about the map case. "Not On here. It's mirages. To the inexperienced, the novice, they appear once or twice a day. Now carry on!"

"But if I might suggest, sir . . ."

"Dammit man, what else could it be but a mirage? What's it look like, eh? Some bloody beggar baked to a crisp sitting in some ridiculous golden throne arrangement! That make any sense at all? You think you're actually seeing that? It's the sirocco, Trout. That, and the foreign food we had to put up with. All right, go on over there. You'll see that it just keeps moving away from you. You'll never get any closer. Go ahead. Only way to learn a lesson!"

The truck edged off the road and navigated the dunes, its tassled flag trembling bravely. Of course it wasn't a mirage, and it didn't go away. The two men, who still proudly wore their uniforms in this foreign land, were greeted at the outset of their mission by a sight of such ingenious savagery, such diabolism, that they immediately inferred from that otherwise barren land a certain kinship. For there in the midst of an inchoate desert—and the place was absolutely pure of any landmarks—was a picked and polished skeleton, its bones baked and creaking in a golden throne that curled into the form of a scorpion. The skeleton glistened dry and clean of everything except some cartilaginous shreds, about which were some live scorpions. There were not many of these. The others, apparently having had their fill, had scattered into the sand. The aluminum bracelet identified their victim as Mr. Ted Stewart. It also swept away the grudging reservations still remaining to the

Division Chief about the case. Heretofore, he could not accept the notion that Dr. Phibes played a part in the Biderbeck matter. Now he could believe nothing else. Phibes it was, and they had to stop him. But his recollection of the way the ubiquitous doctor had manhandled the well-thought-out attempts at his capture at their first meeting was especially sour for Wembley Waverly. He still could not mention that man's name with ease.

"Sir, if I may say so, this also looks to be typically," Trout fumbled for a summation, "typically..."

"Not yet. Don't mention that name to me yet." Waverly cut him off. "This isn't going to work. Have to pick up the whole contraction."

He bent the back of the chair toward the ground. Trout took the legs and together they loaded their grim cargo onto the back of the truck. By their maps Biderbeck's camp was just around the range of small dunes. It couldn't be a happy arrival.

At the moment that the curiously flagged official vehicle bearing his previous evening's handiwork whisked by within a very short radius, Anton Phibes was yet asleep. He languished, as was his habit after similar exertions, in the deep arms of an upright chair. His head, one tousled curl of gray bent along his forehead, rested along a velvet panel. In his hand he held a quarto of his poetry. It was opened to the seventh canto of the "Elegy of Element," one of Phibes' favorites, and the one work that continued to draw very mixed, very partisan comments from the critics.

Vulnavia busied herself in the efficient Pullman kitchen. Her day's cylinder provided specific instructions: he was to be awakened at eleven, at which time he would have a breakfast of shirred eggs, toast squares and fresh strawberries and cream. After breakfast, a witch hazel rub followed by a steam bath. During that period she was to lay out his linen, including his white ruffled shirt and tourmaline jewels bearing the family crest, and brush off his grey morning suit. Finally, she was to prepare the incense and candles for the ceremony.

Vulnavia finished in the kitchen and went to wake Phibes. She took the book and put it on the reading table. Then she looked at him. In repose the lines and hollows were gone from his face. He really did look refreshed and his face, tanned now from the sun, possessed a fresh vigor. She was about to touch him when he opened his eyes and smiled. She caught herself, remembered that what she was seeing was pure cosmetics, but she was elated anyway. At least he *wanted* to look robust—a good sign after the strain of the past months.

Phibes ate quickly, drinking two cups of very dark, very thick Turkish coffee during the process. Then he put on a cylinder of Berber music and went into the bath while Vulnavia busied herself with his wardrobe. Those rapid tribal rhythms were enough to charge the entire apartment, and when Phibes returned he could hear the musicians warming up in the next room. Vulnavia was already gowned in a formal white satin, so he took her arm and, leading the tender girl past the players, marched into the antechamber where his treasured Victoria waited.

With Vulnavia's assistance he removed his wife's precious form from the calliope and, using a silk wrapping sheet to make the transfer, carried her over to the caisson whose wooden bulk had been sheathed in the embossed grey Phibes' burial fabrics. Then, while the musicians launched into Haydn's "Water Music" (they played mandolins for the occasion) Phibes and his charge took up the caisson's white festooned draw bars for their long ascent through the mountain.

The procession marched on stately, yet exuberantly into the mountain. Vulnavia had placed whale oil torches along the path at frequent intervals, and their white smokeless light cast the tunnels in an illumination seen only by the ancient builders of the structure. The wall paintings showed their true colors and Phibes was surprised to see such brilliant reds. From the looks of it, the Egyptians had had an iron ore supply. At least they had known how to work with the metal enough to use it in the pigments.

Elsewhere incense curled out of the censers, bringing a kind of unaccustomed warmth to the damp stone surfaces. The musicians were going through "Water Music" at a somewhat faster rate than usual, and Vulnavia noticed that Phibes' pace was very brisk as a result.

They passed through the ramp intersections and started up. The caisson moved noiselessly and almost without effort on foam rubber tires, with Phibes and Vulnavia in the lead. As always, he walked ramrod straight, cutting a courtly figure in the fine tailored lines of his morning suit. She had strung garlands in her long auburn hair, and could have been a bridesmaid at any royal wedding. The musicians, equally formal in military tuxedos, took up the rear, their mandolins echoing softly in the vast cavernous reaches beyond.

Surprisingly the procession was not out of place. It had been built for a king, and Phibes, in his bearing and dimension, looked completely capable of assuming the part.

They passed through the royal antechamber and entered the gilt-embellished sanctum beyond. At a sign from Phibes the caisson was placed at the base of the sarcophagus. The musicians took up positions in a corner of the splendid room. Then, bowing to her master, Vulnavia circled the room three times, dousing its venerable reaches with perfumed smoke from the censer. Phibes bent his head in supplication before the penultimate moment. Vulnavia returned to his side, plugged a jack from the caisson into his throat, and waited for him to finish his prayer.

After a few moments Phibes opened his eyes to address his beloved. "Victoria, I bring you now to a temporary resting place. Here you shall sleep as if under my own devoted care, awaiting only that moment two days hence, when I shall certainly find the last and final step to the River of Life itself, flowing somewhere inside this mountain. Until then, my sweet queen, sleep your dreamless sleep, and await your true awakening!"

As soon as he finished these words, his voice falling thickly at the end, he grasped the head of the golden snake that curled atop the sarcophagus. At that same moment the musicians stopped playing, held their mandolins down to their sides, and fell silent. Phibes turned the snake's head slightly until it clicked, then he moved it a full half-turn more in the same direction.

The chamber, closed tight countless centuries ago, started to open. It was no accident that its ancient parts, untouched by living hands throughout that enormous span, moved now with ease.

They lifted Victoria and placed her within the sarcophagus' interior. Phibes' hands trembled and mist was in his eye as the cover eased to a close. One last murmured kiss, and he grasped the golden lock and shut it. He turned the half-turn. The lid closed, but not quite. His gloved hand turned again but still a space was left.

The incense curled heavier. The musicians waited for their cue. Vulnavia watched, ever attendant. He could not leave his wife unprotected.

He turned it again. The lid slid back to its ancient confines and was shut.

He turned again, to make sure this time.

Metal ground to metal; there was a persistent, accurate "click" in the silence.

It was the snake's tongue; long, serrated—brilliant in the light glow. He reversed the turn. The tongue retreated. Advanced it, and it came out again. His heart curled to the sense of what was in his hand, the apex to all his plans, all his energies.

The key! The key to the River of Life! Phibes, had he been any other man, would have run thrashing about the myriad passageways in the mountain. The quartz-covered chamber of the moon clock registered two days: two days to find the doorway to that immortal river; forty-eight hours in a half-millennium epoch wherein the entryway emerges from its prearranged occlusion and becomes, as it was in Akhenaton's time, accessible to mortals. It was a sliver of time in which to make the choice between life eternal and nothing at all, a hairline passage of the perennial clockwork to allow him to answer his vow.

But Anton Phibes, as in all things, was a presence unto himself. Just as he had found its key he would find the door, and in plenty of time for his purposes. Supremely in control, he nodded to Vulnavia. The girl circled the chamber three times, again, offering a sweet-scented benediction to their successes, then joined her master. They again picked up the caisson's draw bar for the return processional to their apartments. The two left as they had entered, trailing the now empty carriage behind, with the musicians walking stiffly at its rear. As they entered the descending tunnels the players shouldered their mandolins and were soon racing through an upbeat but miraculously apropos rendition of

"When the Saints Go Marching In."

If there was joy unabated in the mountain there was nought but woe without. The advent of the Trout-Waverly tandem had, as predicted, a devastating effect on the Biderbeck camp. The Arabs, their pragmatic sensitivities already shattered by the discovery of Shavers earlier that morning, looked at the apparition lurking beneath one of their own battle flags and, thinking it to be a ghostly survivor of Omdurman, ran off in one of their own vehicles.

Philo Hackett had fainted and was being treated by Diana, who was also pressed to the extremity by the awful turn of events.

And Biderbeck, whose word and experience had guided the whole enterprise and who could not afford to quit, was being tested more by the Division Chief than by any of the outrageous events prior to Wembley Waverly's arrival. The two men stood now in Biderbeck's big tent. Biderbeck had just presided over Shavers' and Stewart's burials, offering hard, perfunctory words for their last transit, the kind of words one expects under such primitive conditions. Then he sent Diana to one of the smaller tents to regain herself, and invited the men in for a whiskey.

"It seems inevitable, doesn't it?"

"Incredible, abominable, fiendish. Murders are all the same, Mr. Biderbeck. It's the murderers who are different." Waverly's jaw jutted.

Biderbeck was still feeling out the man. "Yes," he added.

"I'm glad you agree with me," Waverly nodded harder.

Trout could see it coming and tried to head off the clash. "If I may capsulize it for you, gentlemen: first Mr. Bruno. Papyrus missing. *Egyptian* papyrus. Second,

Professor Ambrose, overboard from a ship *bound* for Egypt. Third, Shavers, *in* Egypt. Fourth, former Leftenant Stewart *IN* Egypt. Done in by some kind of madman."

"Exactly!"

"But who?"

"You have no idea?" Waverly shot, surprising his subordinate not a little.

Trout, who had never officially been told whether he was on the case or not—in fact he did not know if there *was* a case—sipped his drink and listened.

"I can't imagine anyone who has the same interest in the Mountains of the Dead as I do," Biderbeck was saying.

Trout tried to encourage him. "Do you know of a man called Phibes?"

"Doctor Anton Phibes." Waverly moved it faster. Trout took another drink on that. Biderbeck didn't, or said that he didn't know the doctor.

"Phibes? No, gentlemen, I don't."

"Think hard." Waverly's skin had gotten pink again.

"I think no other way. Who is he?"

"Actually he died," Waverly stumbled a bit, twirled his ice and went on. "We think he did, anyway. But in spite of that..."

Trout jumped to his Chief's aid. "He killed eight men five years ago, all in devilish fashion. He left this life, as the Chief states, but we believe he also is responsible for the deaths of Bruno, Ambrose, Shavers and now Stewart —and that you may be next."

Hackett and Baker, who had been sipping quietly through the banter, didn't like this at all.

"Wait a minute. You trying to tell us about some ghost out there in them mountains, that's come down on our tail just because we've shoveled up a little sand?" Rosemont

Baker leaned up out of his chair. "Because if you are, Inspector, I wonder who's warning them other chaps. Must be fifteen, twenty 'official' groups roaming around this valley, and God knows how many prospectors trying to finish what the grave robbers left."

"But if you're right, sir, I sure as hell want to lay my hands on the bastard. Shavers and Stewart were good men. I know Shavers could've taken care of himself. The bastard that got him must've done it all of a sudden like." Hackett shook his head. "I'd almost like to meet him."

"Well, I'm here to inform you for your own safety that of all these British citizens, you're not going to." Waverly put it right to him.

"What do you mean, sir?"

"I mean that, as I came through Cairo, I was authorized to withdraw your permission to explore in this area by the British ambassador and the Department of Egyptian Antiquities."

"What in hell's name are you talking about?" Biderbeck had it out before he could check himself.

Then Baker started to throw them all in. "You ask me, just as well."

But Waverly's official position started to show its vested powers. "I am empowered to make you strike camp at my discretion, and as a result of my full delineation of the entire Phibes matter, a battalion of British Fusiliers is even now en route by forced march to this very spot to hunt Dr. Phibes, or whoever it may be, and to hunt him out no matter where he is lurking!"

What Biderbeck was hearing was like a goad to a bull. He had to cut the man off. "I don't recognize your authority, sir."

But Hackett was wavering. "Be sensible, man."

So was Baker, who should have acted more loyal than he did. "Think of Diana."

Hackett, who had been, despite the heat and the flies, a good friend of Shavers and who, thinking first about his skin and all that it contained, was ready to pack it in. "Think of all of us, man."

With that Biderbeck promised himself to discharge the man as soon as they finished, but you couldn't tell it from his expression. "You're throwing in the towel? Now, when we're so close?"

"How close are you, Mr. Biderbeck?" Trout seemed curious. Perhaps he would listen to reason.

"We've narrowed it down to a few hundred feet, I know it!"

"From what I gather there's a damn great rabbit warren in those mountains." Waverly wasn't about to let him wriggle loose, not when the lives of British subjects were at stake. "Makes a damn fine hideout. But the Fusiliers'll smoke him out, never fear!"

Biderbeck's voice quivered. That pipsqueak was actually serious. "That 'rabbit warren,' as you call it, is one of the most sophisticated architectural complexes in the ancient or modern world."

But it was no use. Waverly was fully prepared to blow up the whole mountain range if there was evil to be averted. "That won't bother Major Braff and his Scots lads, not at all."

Biderbeck tried to reason. "Sir, I meant to say . . ."

But it wouldn't work. "Oh, the Yard appreciates how you chaps feel about those pots and jugs and bits of bone you dig up."

Biderbeck couldn't listen, got up, poured himself a quick refill, then looked at his men to see how they *did* feel.

"Well?"

"Shavers was my best friend. You know that." Philo Hackett scratched his big belly. The middle two buttons popped, seeming to emphasize his new determination. Biderbeck looked to Baker.

"Old Ted was a bag of wind. But I think somebody's trying to tell us something, and I'm willing to listen."

"Good. We're agreed, then."

Waverly slapped his knee. He always trusted in good common sense.

"You can strike camp first thing after sunup. All travel together. Meet the Major halfway."

"We've *not* agreed, sir," Biderbeck shouted. "Sorry, didn't mean to lose it, but I'd like to ask one consideration."

"Which is?"

"I would like to continue my work until then." When cornered Biderbeck's dedication could be impressive. "With or without anyone else. After all, you two men from the Yard are here to protect us."

It was a devastating shot and it had its desired effect. Waverly actually was mellow when he answered.

"Mr. Biderbeck, *if* you will show good faith and begin striking camp, get the smaller gear packed, I'd be inclined to go along with that. What's the harm, eh? Might come across some pretty beads. No telling what, eh? Keep a sharp lookout of course?"

"Yes, no telling what."

Of course it wasn't in Trout to let it go that easy. "But might I ask, sir, after all, what's so important about two more days?"

But Biderbeck knew the value of silence. Besides, it was time to look in on Diana. He smiled a rather thin, enigmatic smile, and took his leave.

When he got to her tent she was gone. She had probably

returned to her own compartment in the larger main tent. He went back, circling around the rear perimeter to avoid the others. He'd had a bellyful of their nonsense, enough to last him the day. When they got back to London would be time enough to deal with Waverly. He was an insufferable ass, but his superiors would have to impress that character deficiency upon him.

He got to the tent flap of her compartment without being interrupted, but wasn't at all happy about what he saw inside. She was packing and continued to pack as he watched.

"Darling! what are you doing?"

"Getting ready to go back to Cairo, whenever the first vehicle leaves."

"You're *what*? Diana, I know you're upset by what's happened. Anyone would be. But don't leave here now." Biderbeck's reserve, so resourceful minutes ago, now crumbled. She seemed not to notice. "It's not just the deaths. It's everything. This whole experience is something I haven't understood from the very beginning—and I understand even less now."

"I know you're tired and distraught. Of course it's a strain." Biderbeck was casting about.

But she stayed firm. "I'm frightened, yes, but that's not it and you know it. Even now, with all that's happened, you're still not telling me the truth!" She had hit it and went on. "Are you?"

Biderbeck looked, tried to approach her, but couldn't. She was really serious.

"If you don't want to tell the authorities, if you don't want to tell your own men, that's your privilege. But I thought I was different; I thought you loved me."

Biderbeck crumbled a bit more. "I do, you know I do."

But she held on. "I can't believe you any more. Any rational man would leave this horrible place but you insist on staying. And you won't say why. What is here? What's going to happen by tomorrow that won't happen next month or next year?"

Now she did start to weaken. Diana Trowbridge was a gorgeous girl, yet for all her beauty, for all her sheltered, even pampered existence, she had a firm practical grasp of all contingencies that belied a worldliness beneath. But now, perhaps from the deaths as much as from Waverly's crude scare tactics, Biderbeck watched her about to come apart. His heart came into his mouth and he knew that if he couldn't answer her outright he would have to come awfully close.

"Listen to me. I told you in London and I will tell you now. There will come a time when I can tell you everything, when you'll understand everything about me." He almost gave it up. "That will come by sundown tomorrow —either way."

He had said enough. She kissed him

"You're still talking riddles." He kissed her, and once again.

"Have you found the answer to number one yet?" Her voice was very soft now.

"Yes." She kissed him. "Yes, I love you. God knows why, darling, but I do."

Within the hour Biderbeck was leading his diminished but recharged party into the cave network in the mountain opposite. Shavers' surveying had been quite accurate and they were soon into one of the major networks, leaving Waverly and Trout on guard outside, armed with binoculars and fowling pieces, the latter being the best guns possessed by the expedition for long-range firing.

Biderbeck, who led the group at a deliberate, rapid pace, carried a long flashlight and wore an automatic pistol in his belt. Baker and Hackett both had snapped on their service revolvers. Only Diana had ventured in unarmed.

"Not as much moisture, would you say?" They were in a long corridor. Watermarks along the walls indicated that the room had been quite a flood channel at times.

"Water table must be dropping all through the mountain. How did you predict that, sir?" Hackett was beginning to feel good about the whole thing again.

"That's a long story." Biderbeck touched Diana's arm. "You all right?"

"Fine."

They rounded a long curve. Biderbeck raised his arm. "Hold it."

They did.

"Logical place for a boobytrap."

He scouted around, found a chunk of rock and tossed it along the floor ahead of them. It clattered on the stones, coming to a halt against the far wall.

Nothing.

"Probably the next intersection, sir," Baker started ahead. Biderbeck stopped him. "Not yet"

He poked back up the curve while the others waited. When he got back he produced a heavy piece of broken timber. This, too, he threw across the floor. As it crossed a slab the heavy stone depressed a bit, bringing with it an entire section of the roof. Jagged boulders, dust, timbers—all thundered down in an avalanche that would have disposed of a whole platoon of grave robbers.

"I see what you mean, sir." Baker's voice was clipped. But he was ready to stay with Biderbeck as long as he was needed.

Biderbeck was all business. "Come along. If we climb . . ." He was going up the pile of rubble when he stopped and looked off to the side. "Light, quickly!"

The others stumbled and clawed their way up to him. Diana gave him her flashlight, looked as he probed the dust-thickened, dark room, saw there the first flecks of gold, then the outlines of the formal-looking dais on which a coffin—it was larger than that—a sarcophagus rested.

She sensed that this was what Biderbeck wanted, what he had been searching for during the long years of planning and preparation.

She took his hand to enter that immensely quiet chamber. His fingers trembled slightly.

Chapter 9

Wembley Waverly finished his ten paces, selected a metal stake from the pack of them in his kit, and malleted it into the ground. When it was in deep he looped the tripcord under the hook on top, pulled it tight and moved on. Another twenty yards and he had finished. Then to string the tin cans and bits of broken bottles that Trout had collected from the camp's trash heap, set up the flares at each point, and then he could sleep secure that night. Of course he'd have them go to bed with their pistols. Trout's inventory listed two Magnums, a service revolver, Biderbeck's pearl-handled twenty-two, two bird guns, and a brace of *howdahs*. He had never seen one of them before but his Uncle Chumley swore by them. The old boy liked big game. Used to make an annual trip to India after elephants and the big cats.

He tracked a female tiger into a canebrake one day. Got a bullet into her before she disappeared and then went in to finish the job. It was thick and dark inside but he could see from the blood spots that she was still around. She was there, all right, about twenty yards behind him and coming fast. He got off another shot before she jumped but the bullet didn't even drop her. She was in the air by the time he got the *Howdah* out of his belt, but the little cannon did the trick.

Seventy-caliber, it went off like artillery and sent the cat into a sidespin. The thing pushed her so hard it took her shoulder out. She was stone dead when he got to her.

Well, he'd be ready for Mister Doctor Phibes this time. Boobytraps. Armed perimeter firepower. He wished he had some mines and Stokes bombs. He would give the blighter a reception to remember. But the Army boys would take care of that. They'd shake them up out of those tunnels—blast him out if they had to. Then it was the Old Bailey for him. Bring him to justice like the common criminal he was. Give him a taste of the law. He'd testify himself. Introduce the files into evidence. Describe those doctors that looked after Phibes' wife. Fine professional men. Respected in their field. Important to the public welfare. He wished Vesalius was still alive. Keen analytical mind, be an excellent witness for the prosecution. Probably the only one who could explain Phibes' twisted mind. That crazy Biblical idea about the *G'tach*, the ten curses of Pharaoh. The fiend had used eight, killed off the doctors with frogs, bats, ants. The murder weapons read like a bloody zoo. His last victim was Vesalius' own son! But the lads had gotten to the fiend before he could pull it off. There was one more curse to go. Darkness! Whatever the hell that meant, no good could come of it.

Old Bailey would straighten him out and after that, the gallows. Fair trial. Quick decision. And punishment to fit the crime. Be good to have Vesalius' son around. What was his name? Lem? Dropped out of sight after his father passed. No one had heard from him since. Supposed to be off travelling somewhere. The boy could help things along.

Yep, hanging was the only way to settle a man like Phibes. All that business about coming up from the grave stuck in his throat. No scientific basis for it. Besides it was impossible. Problem was, nobody saw him die in the first place. No body, no murder. That's a legal axiom—or was it? They would have saved a lot of trouble if they had made sure the first time. He always had the notion that Phibes was still somewhere around the Maldine Square building. Wouldn't have requested that permit to dismantle the place if he didn't. But it took the building people three years to get around to the paperwork. Place was always crawling with sightseers. He suspected the press as having their finger in it. Wanted to embarrass him. Make it look bad for the Department. Every so often they would trot out that "Elusive Killer" story to keep the public excited. Even spelled his name wrong. And by the time they did get around to pulling the walls down, Phibes could have been in the Arctic.

That was all over with now. Wherever Phibes went, he was quiet about it, but he made the mistake of coming back. Even the smartest criminals do that. A bunch of egotists, the lot of them. Come back just in time to make one last mistake, Phibes was just like the rest, and he would pay like the rest of them.

Waverly strung the last of the tin cans into the trip wire, picked up his bird gun, and stepped back a bit to check his work. The cord stretched completely around the camp at knee level. There were enough tin cans hanging on it to wake the dead if anyone tripped the wire. Everything was worked out after that. He had given Trout explicit instructions to send a flare barrage up as soon as he heard the wire. Then he was to blow his whistle in short bursts till the others were out of their tents, and assembled around Biderbeck's big tent. Each man was assigned a fire zone so that approach from any angle was impossible. To make it more difficult he had had Hackett and Baker extend the latrine trench around the big tent. Six jerry cans of petrol were stored inside. If things got too rough Trout and one of the men were instructed to flood the latrine channel with petrol and fire it. He liked to call it their "thermal barrier," behind which they could make their stand until Braff and his Fusiliers arrived on the scene. He had ordered provisions to be laid out: beef jerky, biscuits, water, and several big tins of lemon sours, which for some reason had turned up in one of the trucks. It was enough to last three days, plus ammunition, enough for one hundred rounds per man per day, and a case of daytime flares in the event the Fusiliers wandered off course.

Waverly took another look around the camp and felt a tot of satisfaction. The string trip wire made everything much neater, much more containable. The camp *looked* secure. He hefted his rifle, wet the sights with his thumb, and took dead aim at the moon. Then he shouldered his gun and walked back toward the camp.

The others were all in one of the smaller tents when Waverly got back. Biderbeck had bunged one of the Watneys and Diana was pouring drinks all around from a foaming pitcher. Even Biderbeck had gotten with it. He was up on the truck bed with that stone casket they found, hopping about like a kid with a new toy. Only Trout was missing; probably out cleaning the pistols.

"Hip, hip," Baker piped through his suds.

"Hooray!" They were relaxing and ready to celebrate. Diana reached up to fill Biderbeck's metal cup. Then he raised it for the toast.

"I thank you. But this is *my* toast to all of you who made this possible. Those here and those departed." He nodded toward the sarcophagus and downed his cup. Another round of applause and Waverly thought he had better remind them of their deadlines.

"All I can say is that I'm delighted you found this very handsome," he spoke in his most winning manner, "archaeology item. And that now all of us can return to civilization with mission accomplished per schedule, per promises, and per request. Right, sir?"

That last was for Biderbeck. "As you say, Inspector. But there's a great deal to be done before we leave, gentlemen. It's very late, I know you're all hungry and, as it happens, you're going to have a treat. Instead of an Arab chef, we're privileged to have Diana as a volunteer. You may end up with watercress sandwiches but it's worth a go."

"That sounds like a cue," Diana laughed.

"I'm afraid it is. Now if you'll all start I'll be along."

Waverly escorted Diana. Hackett grabbed a keg. Baker gathered the cups and was on his way out when Biderbeck stopped him.

"Rosemont, I'm going to move ahead here. If you could bring me something for a snack?"

"Righto."

"And I wonder if you'll take the post watch in here when I go to bed? Could you move your cot in?"

"Absolutely. I'll spell off with Hackett at midnight?"

"Thanks."

Baker nodded at their prize.

"She's a beauty, eh, sir?"

"Probably the greatest find of the century. If I can unravel all the secrets locked in there, it will be more important than Tut-Ankh-Amon. Perhaps more important than the Rosetta Stone. I think there can be more knowledge gained from *this* than from any other work in all of man's history."

"That's a little beyond me, sir," he started out. "This

what Dr. Phibes is after, too?"

"I suppose so."

"But why?"

"If I knew *exactly*, half my work would be done."

Baker had been juggling the cups to get them in a stack, shuffling and balancing them in his thick fingers in what looked like a futile effort to Biderbeck. He finally managed some kind of equilibrium and clattered out.

At last Biderbeck was alone with his prize. It had been an enormous temptation for him to spill it all back into the mountain. After all, in their view and anyone else's who cared to look hard enough, Jonathan Biderbeck had a record, a reputation that stood for something more than flim-flam. He was one of the few who planned and backed his own expeditions. He was meticulous. He played by the rules, and he usually came up with the "big find." It would have been simple, even honorable, to disband after Ambrose's death; certainly after the death of Shavers.

But he hadn't told them *why* he was going on, and he didn't know if he would after the work was finished. A few hours ago the planning, the expense, the dangers, and the awful waiting found its own reason when they broke into that hidden chamber in the mountain. He knew when he saw the sarcophagus for the first time that his search was nearing a conclusion. It was enough that Diana knew it as well.

He looked at the sarcophagus for several long moments, registering its most minute dimension as one would a meteor or some such object from the heavens. Then he touched it, recording to his touch that which his eyes beheld. His hands ran in an infinitude of rhythms along its bottom, top, and sides. He had not taken his eyes off of it from the first but he still couldn't get enough of it.

Of course the snake head was more than an ornament. The glyphs along the upper surface hinted at its importance but he would have to spend several hours with them before he could have a rough translation. He stroked the head and tail. The surfaces were cold to the touch. But wait! He felt movement. Parts inside were moving! An internal mechanism was counting!

He pressed the head and simultaneously with it, the tail, a fraction of a turn clockwise. There were two immediate results. The snake's head parted slightly to slowly emit a serrated solid gold tongue, and the top lid of the sarcophagus rose. Inside, on a bed of faience myrtle leaves, lay the most elaborate mummy case Biderbeck had ever seen. It would have been easy, awfully easy for Biderbeck to simply pry open the inlaid casing. Royal mummies often had two or three outer cases and as many layers of cloth wrappings. The whole, being wood and cloth, was installed in the sarcophagus further to protect the personage within. But Jonathan Biderbeck was too disciplined a scholar. The mummy was probably a member of the royal household, possibly Akhenaton himself.

At the very least he would have to catalog the various layers as well as the contents of the sarcophagus and its lining. Then he must study the figure itself, measure it, describe its condition and photograph it. He had read enough of the contemporary descriptions of that Pharaoh to feel competent in making a determination. He would leave verification up to the museum crowd. They could argue over what they had for as long as they wanted! They'd get a clean set of notes from him!

He put his surgical instruments into the autoclave and laid out the larger instruments on a tray near the sarcophagus. He planned to remove the wooden casings, photograph them, and then set them aside for later study. Then he would take off each cloth layer separately, using sterile technique. He didn't want to chance contaminating the mummy. He planned to photograph and measure the mummy itself, depending on its condition, before sending it on.

He opened the large red leather-bound notebook to a section of fresh pages inserted past the midpoint. There, on the sheet just after the tab, he made the first entry: "June 5, 1931, Tell-el-Amarna."

It was after nine when Biderbeck finished work. The outer wood casing, beautiful as it was, offered little information other than that its occupant was a member of the royal court. The second casing, also of wood, was more provident. Biderbeck started to read it, then became so absorbed that he worked through the entire translation of what developed to be a delineation of her immortal love by Pi Ankhi's concubine. Pi Ankhi had been the Pharaoh's Chief Servitor.

> I would rather have spoken this to you, my lord, but to get close enough so that only your ear commands the privacy of my lips requires risks best reserved for our couplings. Favorite as these heavenly moments are, they have been too few and infrequent in the extreme, sufficiently infrequent so that my chest gathers its sweet lovely pain. My eyes cloud in absence of their most excellent estimate and my legs ache in the emptiness of your weight. You, my loved one, have too many wives. Too many wives! I repeat it so you will not misunderstand my intent. It was in innocence that I loved you first. At age eight, innocence is a practical shield to the world. I saw you that year on my birth date; saw you and didn't speak. You will not remember the small party given in my honor. You were a very important man even then and you had much business about the palace. You were always

hurrying about so. But you were kind enough to pay your respects to our little gathering. You touched my cheek and I never forgot the softness and strength of your fingers. That night I wanted to ask my parents to offer me to your service as a wife. Fear and perhaps a little bit of modesty restrained me from blurting out the feelings in my small heart.

After that, I tried to get a glimpse of you whenever I could. You were very handsome to me. Your walk was unlike other men's; you seemed always to have something important to do. During times of difficulty you were calm. When others were idle, you were purposive. And when there was much merrymaking and carousing, you kept your head.

When I was ten you gave me a present of some bracelets you brought back from Eleqon. Since that city is very far away I thought you had gone to much trouble to please me, and I was certain in my secret heart that you loved me. Only later did I learn that it was your duty to visit this Asiatic place, and Byblos, Ascalon, Tyre, as well as Thebes and Herakleopolis.

At twelve I gave you a present, a present which, it has been taught to me, a girl reserves for the one she loves most in life. I confess now that I employed a ruse on that day, and that when I invited you into my bath you may not have known my purpose, but I certainly did.

Did you rest well that night? I have always wanted to ask you that, my sweet lord.

I was convinced we would marry presently; so convinced that I caused a marriage gown to be made for me, and I taught myself how to make those sweetcakes you like. I prayed that you would take me to Eleqon in celebration of our troth.

A month later I learned that you *did* marry—to a woman noisier and more irascible than your first two wives.

You may remember that I didn't speak to you after that, and that my silence lasted nearly thirty days.

Your fourth wife was worse yet; she of the fat lip and bulbous shanks. Her voice charged the palace halls, and her feet made them shake. I was told that she helped your position, that her money and contacts caused you to be elevated in the eyes of the others at court. When I heard this my heart was sad.

That year I travelled to Abydos with my sister. We left when the wheat fields were coming new green. The river was high then and the boat moved very fast. That entire trip was a memory of my love for you. The ship's white sail registered its purity; the whirlpools, its turbulence; the long-flowing Nile, its timelessness. Now Abydos is a busy city, filled with couriers, craftsmen, traders and farmers, and my uncle, who is not a poor man, treated his nieces with consideration befitting his rank. He brought us to meet many of the older families of the city where we were graciously received and made welcome. Parties were given in our honor and the young men came calling. During the day my sister and I went to the markets; just to look at all the bright cloths was an entertainment. On special occasions we sailed out on the Nile on a marvelous barge to an island upstream where the wealthy merchants kept pleasure lodges. Oh, my lord, I should be mortified if I were to tell you what went on in those places, but modesty prevents me from describing those activities which these people pursued so actively. I was thankful that my dear aunt and my sister acted as chaperones—not that anything would tempt me into these lewd behaviors.

"Sir?"

"Oh, Rosemont, it's you!" Biderbeck looked up from his work. "What time is it?"

"About nine. I brought your sandwiches. Miss Trowbridge asked if you didn't mind not having watercress and will smoked turkey do? She sure can cook fine."

Biderbeck checked his own watch. He'd been working two hours! Gotten so wrapped up in that love letter that the night had just about slipped by. "Here, put them down. Did you have enough to eat?"

"Stuffed as a Christmas hen. The little lady filled the table up with sandwiches and hot beef soup. Sure beats them nuts and oranges the Arabs were feeding us. Those two police chaps turned in 'bout an hour ago. Chief Waverly gave me this and told me to keep it on tonight."

"But that's your own gun, Rosemont."

"I know. Trout collected all the weapons after we got back from the mountain. Said something about our arsenal."

"So that's what he was doing."

"What, sir?"

"He popped in here when I was shaving, asked if I had a gun, and if I didn't mind wearing it. I told him mine was on the desk. He took the serial number, mumbled something about security, and slipped out."

"Funny birds, those cops."

"Well, I suppose they try hard enough to do right. They don't get paid all that much, so it must be the dedication."

"You don't say, sir? Now I read somewhere that the boobies made a decent living. Decent enough to pay the rent and buy the groceries."

"I'm sure you're right, Rosemont, but they're in a risk business. Protect the public. Apprehend dangerous criminals." He noticed that Baker was still standing. "Rosemont, do sit down. Have a drink if you like. I'll just be a bit longer here and then I'll turn in."

Baker put the tray down on the table next to the sarcophagus and slid into one of the camp chairs. "Well, just long enough to have a smoke and go. Hackett's over there all alone with an open keg. He was already afloat when I left. You'd think with that big belly he could hold his liquids, but two cups and the man is drunk.

" 'Dronk,' as Pepys called it but not sotted. Fat people

usually eat more than the rest of us, which means they can drink more, too. The food acts as a sponge so they're more apt to be 'dronk' than to become tumbledown tosspots."

"You're right on that, sir. I never saw old Hackett actually stumble over himself, but he can put it away like he's got holes in his legs."

"He's an experienced eater. We had to provision as much for him and Ambrose as for the rest of the party combined."

"He was a fine man and a gentlemen, sir. Didn't know the Professor that well myself but the others called him 'fair.' Good to work for. Even the Arabs seemed to like him. Awful way to go!" Baker fished a dark Italian cigar from his pants pocket, bit the dry stub end off, and lit it with a sulfur match. The tent quickly blossomed with the heavy wine-soaked fumes. He drew hard until the cigar tip was cherry red. Then he leaned across the desk. "I'll tell you this, sir, them two biscos better look sharp hereabouts. Any bloke slick enough to pack the Professor in a gin bottle got to have a lot more tricks where that came from. And if he's the same guy that did in old Shavers, he's a mean customer to boot. Why Shavers was a hard gangster. Ran a pack of whores up in Bristol before the war. They said he killed a coupla punks over a skirt. Carried a shiv long as your arm under his belt. You couldn't pay me to tangle with that sonuvabitch. So whatever somebody got to him *must've* been pretty tough!"

"Shavers got careless. Then he got bushwhacked. Waverly told me about his special security arrangements. Said he was in Intelligence during the war. Seems to know what he's doing."

"Yeah, I heard about that 'thermal barrier' too. Flare guns and whistles to scare 'em off. But this ain't the Western Front. That's why I got me some extra insurance." Baker patted a bulge along the edge of his trousers.

"What's that you have there, Rosemont?"

"Little equalizer the non-coms used on night patrols. Good in an ambush. Could take a squad out in close quarters." He slid the piece on to the table. A double-barrelled shotgun sawed off to about eighteen inches overall, it looked intimidating.

"Do the others know about that, Rosemont?"

"No, and I'm not going to tell 'em. It's always good to have a little ace in the hole." He hefted the gun and slid it back in his trousers. "I'll be getting back now, Mr. Biderbeck. Like I said, you can't leave old Hackett alone too long with a keg. Put the whole thing away, he would, and where would we be tomorrow?"

"I guess you've got him pegged. You'll be back in about an hour then?"

"Oh yes. Now that we've found what we've been looking for, we damn well better take care of it. I'll see that the old bastard don't get too soused up to stand his watch. You can count on that, sir."

"I know I can. Good night, Rosemont."

When the man left Biderbeck went back to his translation . He was anxious to see Diana. It was like a timelock with him! If he didn't have her close he felt oddly tired, diminished. But he wanted to finish that translation first. It was only the outpourings of a young girl's heart but he felt that something was contained there, something terribly important to his final push into the mountain. He adjusted the lamp, bent closer to the gold symbols, and continued his notes.

> I will confess that several of the younger men in my uncle's circle did come calling. Most of them came for my sister. She is a year older, and I thought prettier than me.

Often we sang for them, and my sister would do a dance occasionally, although not at all immodest. They were really very attentive, especially one young man who was the son of a priest at Re's temple. He seemed very learned, very spiritual. Often he would come early in the morning and ask me to go on long walks with him to watch the sun rise. He liked to read hymns to Re at that hour and his voice was indeed fervent. He always walked ahead of me, chanting in that very deep voice of his out over the water's edge. No one was about except the onagers, which ran off whenever we got too close. When he was done be would wait for me to catch up with him and often there would be tears in his eyes.

Oh, my lord, the young man did ask to visit me after I returned home. I even think he would have wanted to speak to my parents. Of course, he was so spiritual I couldn't really tell. I told him that I was promised to another. I hope you do not mind. We did go walking after that but his chanting didn't seem so strong.

It was harvest time when my sister and I returned to Amarna and the wheat was very brown in the fields. I trembled in my room that night, thinking of being so close to you, and yet unable to look at you. It was so long that I was away.

I'm afraid I was a bit too impatient in our greeting the next morning. But I could tell by your expression, by your unquiet eyes, that you had missed me. My sister remarked later that I did dismiss her rather sharply, and I had to explain to her several times that the trip had left me in great need of a refreshing bath. You, of course, told me how busy you had been, of your mission to Nubia and the great buildings going up in Amarna. But you weren't too busy to slip into the bath after my sister had left. Receiving your noble log felt like a part of me had returned to my body. I hope I did not cry out too loud.

My doubts of your devotion truly vanished during the next few months. When I awoke you were at the edge of my bed. In the evening you were in my bath, and during the day we managed to find each other in a hundred different ways. When I asked why you felt it necessary to see me that often, I was only teasing. But I'm still puzzled over your answer. Why did you say it was because I have grown up?

I think I have loved you as strongly at eight as at eighteen, for you are as much a king in my eyes now as you were then, second only to our great lord Akhenaton in the reverence of the earth and the gods. Had we never met I would have preserved the vision of your strength, of your firm and worldly wisdom in my innermost heart. We all need someone to believe in, someone to hold above all others. Then, as now, you are my model.

It is said that Amarna is a new expression on earth, an expression of the Aton, a single god who is Lord of the heavens and of all men. It is said that Pharaoh is Aton's son, that the guide is in his guise. And it is said that not all men know the truth of Aton and that we have many enemies.

I know very little of such things called diplomacy and politics, my lord. I understand only that when one is hungry one needs to eat, when one is cold one should find shelter. All the rest that I know is about love.

But I have heard that some men overstep themselves, that they want more than they have, or imagine that others have taken what is rightly theirs. And that to keep a balance between these people who are dissatisfied with their lot and all the rest of the others has been offered as a definition of politics. If so, yours is a very difficult job. Even in my humble position I have heard of the envy showered upon our city by other places in the land. There are rumors about that not everyone worships Aton as a single god of the heavens. And there are less pleasant rumors still—oh my lord, will you be upset with me? But it is said that our most noble and sacred Pharaoh is not admired equally by all of his subjects. In fact, there are some that revile the king and plot against him.

Yours is a difficult job, my lord. I have seen it in the furrow of your eyes, felt it when you sigh against my breast. Lately I find myself worrying about you.

My lord, forgive me for being so direct, but I think you to be ill-served by your wives. They have allowed you to become fatigued without affording you a remedy within the confines of your apartments. They have permitted you to go out to business with your robes frayed. They have not fed you properly, as I can tell by the odor that sometimes comes from your mouth. And they harass you. Don't deny it; they are worrisome and shrill. I can see it in your tics, in the clearings of your throat, in the wistful ness of your eyes.

Sire, you are a great man, a noble and busy man. I suspect that our glorious Pharaoh leans heavily on you, and that your shoulders are always willing to bear the burdens of this heavy office. Certainly you love your king as much as any citizen, more so than most.

Then why do your wives not care for you? Are they jealous of your abilities? Then let them take up singing and the dance. Are they indolent in the management of the house? Then they should instruct the servants you have so graciously provided, or find new ones. Do they displease you in bed? But do not answer that!

My sister has recently given me a small amulet that she found cast into our quarters by a strange hand. She was frightened by it and I have had to calm her. When I conveyed its contents to you it was only out of the belief that your great wisdom and the gentleness of your heart would control any exigencies.

"Tef Tef, born to Hotep, and daughter of Pa Nehri, shall die." I do not want to die, my lord, I am happy with my lot I've harmed no one nor do I covet that which is not mine. My singing and dancing are pleasing to the eye, or so I have been told. I have not dishonored my parents, have been loyal to friends and helpful to strangers. Mostly I do not want to be away from you.

My dear sweet lord, your response as always has been more than I could ask. Rather than cast me off in the face of this threat—and we will not name its source—you have taken me closer into your life. Whereas before I found myself content to idle through the long hours of the day, waiting for the evening when you could at last be in my bath, I find myself rushing, actually rushing so that I can visit you in your new work. I hurry, taking care to be seen by as few people as possible, toward the docks where your boatswain always waits at the appointed place. The trip over the river is always much longer than the one back.

The first day I must admit I was confused by the site to which your map had led me. It was a mountain, undistinguished from several others around it. Only after I had entered and passed through its myriad corridors and apartments did I realize the wonder of the place. I have visited Thebes with my parents and this surpasses anything built in that place. If I may say it, I think the noble memory of Akhenaton, son of Aton, whose works he made strong on earth, will be well served by the memorial you have organized for him.

After that first day I could not wait to see the wondrous thing you were doing, to be near you. And I noticed you were growing stronger, my lord. Your chest was an an iron shield above me just as your shank felt as an iron when you clove within me. Again I have a confession to make, my lord. I'm afraid that the heat in my belly overcame my discretion, but one day, out of curiosity, I equipped myself with an hourglass. When I reached the chamber you had assigned for our meeting, I lay it on its side behind the pillows, unfastened my gown and lay back on the pillows awaiting your arrival. Presently you did come, and as soon as you ungirdled your armor and made that first sweet shove of your stalwart craft into my harbors, which were even then delirious with their own waiting, I reached behind the pillows —your face was in my hair—and placed the hourglass on its end. My lord, do you know that when you next exited from me after our visit to the heavens, the hourglass had run out?

Yet you are gentle in your ferocity. Just as you have provided for us in life, you have made all accommodations for us after death. Your promise that we will be together when that time comes is all that my small heart requires.

The day you described our course past the grave you were bound up with great trepidation even as you spoke. I know that your circumstances are most pressing, my lord, and I wish that I could help you more than my ability. But be assured that I have instructed my most trusted maid fully on what to do in the event of my passing. She is to place the lozenge you provided beneath my tongue. Then she is to summon Sekeret, the emissary of your secretary. He will see that I am conveyed to our great Pharaoh's tomb, to be placed there in the vault you have selected for me. At the appropriate time the lozenge will awaken me from permanent sleep. I will then pass along the corridors you have so carefully demonstrated to the gates of immortality at the end of the farthest chamber to the East. There, using the snake's head key, I will enter those doors. Beyond you have moored a boat on the River of Life. And, as I have done so many times in the past, I will float toward the Island of Heaven and Earth, there to meet with you and begin our eternal love.

Akhenaton has graciously provided you, the most trusted of his servants, with an elixir that will gain these fondest dreams.

Then, as now, I will await you calmly.

And oh, my lord, I have caused this to be placed above my remains so that others will know how well our love has served us. I hope my impudence will not discomfort you.

Chapter 10

Jonathan Biderbeck finished the young girl's testament just before midnight, troubled by both her fate and her faith. He replaced the two wooden coverings and the sarcophagus top as well, and was studying the golden snake when he heard footsteps beyond the tent. He just had time to snap off its head when Baker slouched in.

"Rosemont! What are you doing here?"

"Well, uh, I came back like you told me." Baker's voice seeped out somewhat thickly. He stumbled, rather than walked toward the camp stool. "You know that muckling bastard Hackett is out?"

"Out? What d'you mean he's 'out'?"

"I said it. Swacho, slammo, out!" Baker peered at Biderbeck. "He knocked the keg off."

"Ah!"

"With a bit of help. I couldn't let the man down. Besides, the bugger was starting to sing, and I didn't want him to disturb Miss Diana and those two coppers."

"Are they all right?"

"Sounder'n bedbugs. The little lady cleared up the mess and retired in good form. And the two bluecoats went out to 'look at the perimeter.' They were snoring through the flap when I passed."

"And Hackett? He's all right?"

"I said he's all right. He's just drunk is all, or 'dronk,' like the good Mr. Pepys would have it."

"What did you do with him?"

"I didn't do nothing. The keg did it all. Opened him, folded him and put him down. He's in his cot now, sir, but I don't think he'll be able to stand his watch."

"Well, that isn't good, is it, Rosemont?"

"It's not good, it's too good, because the old fart can't see for shit anyway."

"Rosemont! Hackett's your colleague."

"Colleague and friend—but he still can't see for shit. I've told him as much to his face.
Without his specs he ain't worth a plugged nickel."

"That's different. Thought he hurt his eyes. He was all right in the tunnel today. Where are his glasses?"

"He sat on 'em!"

"Well, how in God's name did he?"

"Sat on 'em with his big fat ass. The keg had him, Mr. Biderbeck, sir. He was *'dronk.'* Sniveling and belching so bad that the others had to leave. And he said to me, he said: 'Baker, we been pushed. We been pushed with the good Doctor Ambrose, bless his rosy cockles. Pushed with Stewart. You,' he says to me, 'you know, Baker, I couldn't stand that shithandle. He used snuff!!' Now you'll pardon me, but these's Hackett's own words. He says: 'I couldn't stand that shithandle Stewart, but I respected him. You know why?' "

"Why?"

Baker whistled and gargled on. "Hackett says, 'Because he worked for Mr. Biderbeck. Worked for him hard. But we were most awfully pushed when my good and clean friend—a man I ate with, slept in the same patch of sand with, pissed against the same palm tree with, that saintly asshole Shavers—why did they have to kill him? A good man and true. One you could laugh with, drink with, even trust your poke with. I'll tell you I'm going to put the clam on that bisco. He's mine. I'm going to take him myself for what he did to my friend. You— and I know you will—have to promise to me that if you snag the one that did it, he's mine. Five minutes is all I want and then you've got the rest of him.'"

"Then he shook my hand, sir, and sat down. Right on his specs. I put him into his cot and came right down here. I don't think old Hackett will be up to much for the rest of the evening. So if you don't mind, Mr. Biderbeck, I've brought a book along with me equalizer. When the one runs out, the other'll take over."

"Is Hackett all right otherwise, Rosemont?"

"Other than a bloody set of hams he's okay. Had to pick a few splinters out of him. He'll be red hot in the morning. Told me those specs set him back ten quid."

"I guess you're it then, Rosemont. I'm going to turn in. Be a busy day tomorrow. Got to finish up in the mountain. Maybe some fairly difficult tracking. Soon as we're done we can break out the champagne."

"Please don't mention that, sir. My poor old guts got to take me through the night yet."

"Then it's goodnight. Look after things here, won't you, old man?"

"Count on it, sir, and goodnight to yourself."

Biderbeck trotted out with enough kick in his step to knock a horse down. Probably was going to jump that little lady of his. He had heard them that morning, rattling around the tent enough to make the damn thing fall down.

But that was all right. A man was only as good as he could screw. Old Biderbeck paid them top dollar and, judging from that heifer's screams, he was tops in that department too. Well, enough of those kinds of ideas. He hadn't seen a skirt lifted in six weeks, ever since he had banged that little redhead the night he left Galveston. She was one piece of all right; jumped on his pintle like she was trying out for the Olympics. He couldn't figure it out, but he always liked it better lying on his back. Girls seemed to like it, too. Gave 'em more room to maneuver and be themselves. Besides it was fun to watch them bounce and jump with their jugs flying around the same way their hair was going. He liked to diddle 'em until he could see the heat rising, then spin 'em around and make 'em race the other way. That always knocked him out. He used to whack 'em on their meatwagons until they were screaming good and proper, then he'd stick his fist in the lady's mouth and ride her home. Women acted better when you treated them rough.

Bigod, he better not think about it. Six weeks was a long time. The book would take his mind off it. And it was going to be a long night.

Biderbeck cut catty-corner across the camp toward his tent. Save for Baker's the tents were dark, their flaps knotted against the night air. The trucks were all lined up, dusted, serviced and ready for the pullout. Overall rose the flagpole with the colors spread softly in the bright wind. Like all of his other missions, the camp bore out his emphasis on planning and execution according to a timetable. He didn't believe in mistakes, at least not on his side of the line. Control meant knowing when to apply the pressure and how much, and despite the setbacks on this trip, they were ready for the payoff.

He was two-thirds of the way across when he heard

some heavy padded feet, an odd sound at an odd time. Turning and drawing at the same time, he already had a bead when Trout's call stopped him.

"Hey!"

"Trout! You gave me a scare." Harry Trout loped the last few paces to join Biderbeck. He was wearing a grey sweat shirt and from the looks of his forehead, had been running at a good clip.

"Only way to . . . get the kinks . . . out."

"That's what the books say. Lucky for both of us you called out when you did. You almost caught it." Biderbeck slid the .22 back in his belt holster.

"I guess I did make a pretty good target. Full moon. Security situation."

"Your chief put that into effect and I can't say I blame him. Your Dr. Phibes sounds like some sort of a magician. What do you know about him?"

"Too much. And not enough. Gave us a big turn about five years ago. A bunch of prominent physicians. Somebody had it in for 'em. A regular vendetta. Pulled it off, too. Most ingenious. The 'Plagues of Pharaoh.' You must have read about it."

"In London, 'Twenty-five, or maybe it was 'Twenty-six. Of course! If I'm not mistaken the killer was never brought in. Seems that there was also some speculation that he never existed, although I couldn't figure that one out at the time." Biderbeck looked at Trout. "So *that* was Phibes! But how did you know? I mean, don't you have to establish identity, motive and the like?"

"He had a motive, all right. His wife died in surgery. Those doctors plus one nurse were on the team that did her in."

"And you didn't pick him up?"

"He was dead."

"Dead? He sounds more like a victim than a criminal. Unless I was right the first time. A magician sounds close to the mark."

"Oh, it was in his official report. Car crash in France. Death by incineration."

"That sounds final."

"Absolutely. But the *Sûreté* never located the remains."

"They're pretty thorough. What made you so sure you had a prospect? I mean, other than a good motive?"

"That part was easy enough. We checked out the family crypt at Knightsbridge. His niche was dated and sealed, but empty. So was his wife's."

"Then there were two missing bodies?"

"And seven dead doctors. And one nurse, of course."

"Of course."

"Could it have been anyone else?"

"That didn't matter. At least, by the time we got fully involved it didn't matter."

"You mean somebody was caught napping? And I had always taken comfort in the fact that the Department was efficient, vigilant, resourceful."

"And organized. Of course in your line you aren't too much concerned with channels and chains of command, Mr. Biderbeck."

"If you believe that, you believe that the pyramids were put up just to store the pottery they contain. Obviously you've never had to deal with research committees, foundations, and the secretaries that stand guard over such things."

"Red tape. No way to get around it. But to answer your question, what started out as a curious murder case was something else again by the time we could break loose the manpower to go after it."

"And then it was too late."

"That is rather hard to believe."

"The *G'Tach* was half through before we'd assigned guards to prospective victims."

"The *G'Tach*? That's Old Testament stuff."

"Exodus. One of the details that led me to Phibes."

They'd been walking around the string perimeter. Biderbeck paused at this revelation and looked at the detective.

"Among his other achievements, Phibes had taken a doctorate in theology at Oxford." Trout answered Biderbeck's glance.

"What else did the talented doctor do?"

"Oh, the other degrees were in physics and music. Didn't have to work. Family was Austrian. Old money. Land. More recently import-export. His youth was, for want of a better word, squalid. He floated through his classes performing adequately, nothing more except for an occasional fleck of brilliance."

"A perennial student."

"Until Victoria Regina entered the picture."

"His wife?"

"And nurse, lover, saint and magnet. She brought him, a wastrel of forty, out of decadence, and turned him into one of the hardest-working, most resourceful public servants the Crown has ever enjoyed. In fact, that's why he was away when she died. He travelled a lot, was known in the foreign service as a man to be counted on."

"I'm still puzzled. You say you never saw him? No one had ever seen him since the doctors started dying," Biderbeck was agitated, "and yet Phibes becomes a killer?"

"You said it right there, Mr. Biderbeck. He *became* a

killer. A brilliant public man who had so much lost it all when his young, gorgeous wife dies. He comes apart. Decides that her 'killers' must die. And does it."

"Without him you can't prove it!"

"Without him we can't prove anything!! As I said, by the time we got involved it was immaterial. We put up quite a show toward the end—twenty-four-hour security and all that. But our man got through and did his business. On number eight we got lucky. Tracked him to a big brownstone on Maldine Square where he'd taken Dr. Vesalius' son. Vesalius was merely a consultant on the case but I guess that put him in the charmed circle."

"Was it Phibes? The man you tracked?"

"Someone who looked like him."

"How's that?"

"A look-alike. There was a mask. Awful ruckus getting to him. Had a gang of clockwork musicians who gave our boys a terrible time. And a young girl. His assistant of sorts. Used an axe like the best of the Vikings."

"Did you nab him or not?"

"Not. Trick elevator in the organ. Had Vesalius and the boy downstairs. Acid bath. Key implanted under the heart. Made the man take it out himself. Aged him fifty years. Didn't last one more."

"Did the boy live?"

"Oh, yes. We got to 'em as quick as we could get by the rear guard on the upper level. Vesalius had the boy. But no Phibes."

"Vanished! Convenient, I'd say."

"We took the place apart. Nothing. Vesalius did say something about a mask and a skull head, but it was a blank. Even pulling the building down a few years later turned up blanks."

"Mr. Trout," Biderbeck's tone had a new edge, "what the hell are we doing here?"

Trout didn't pick up on it right away. Biderbeck nodded at the string.

"What's all this paraphernalia about? You've been talking about a man, an officially *dead* man, who apparently has walked away from a fatal automobile accident, returned to England without notice, and wiped out a pack of medicos by your own admission. A fairly aggressive manhunt, climaxed by a head-to-head knockdown after which he permanently vanished!?" He waited for it to register. "What the *hell* are we doing? I mean, cans on a string, whistles and Very pistols! Sir! Do you want to frighten the man or capture him? If, indeed, such a man as Phibes exists, and *is* here."

"Mr. Biderbeck, there *are* other explanations," Trout was feeling his vinegar, "or do we need . . ."

"On the contrary, I won't deny that this mission has been dogged by some 'unfortunate' accidents. At this late hour it serves no one to get caught in definitions, except the essential ones. I believe that there *is* a Phibes. And that he's out there in the sand somewhere. What I don't believe is that these 'trinkets' are going to do much of anything in the way of preventing the man from getting on with his obsession, which seems to be killing us all off."

"Major Braff will be here tomorrow."

"Threat or promise, Mr. Trout? If the best-trained detection and prevention body in Western civilization could not deter this gifted criminal, I doubt that if it were Field Marshal Braff of the head of an army group the results would be very much different."

"I believe, sir, that Chief Waverly would take offense at that"

"Inspector, that man, I am sure, is dedicated as the cuffs

in his trousers, and his concern for the public weal cannot be questioned. After all, he is a popular lecturer on the good works of the Department, is he not?"

"Very much so, sir!"

"And this was his plan?"

"Chief Waverly, as my superior, was in charge of the original case."

"So he wants to change his luck—with Phibes, that is?"

"I would think so, sir."

"And he sincerely believes he's following a provident course. I mean he thinks that he's got a new crack at the scoundrel and this time he's going to follow through."

"The Chief is very persistent." They reached Biderbeck's tent.

"Mr. Trout, please excuse my directness, but tell me, what do *you* think?"

"I think we've got a shot at it, sir."

"You don't seriously believe that all of this," he nodded at the string, "is going to make one tot of difference to Phibes? If it's him who is out there?"

"I said I think we've got a shot at it. It would be a better one if you'd tell us why you're really here."

Biderbeck started. "I don't think I have to go over my credentials."

"That's not what I mean, sir. Your excellent work in Egypt and other places is part of the record. But I don't think you've come here to excavate old mountains—even if they do contain hidden burial chambers."

"Akhenaton was among the greatest Pharaohs. He founded a city, established a revolutionary religion, and turned the culture around. Many other scholars have been interested in him."

"And none have had as much luck, good and bad, as

you. There's another factor—a 'variable,' to use your parlance. You're after it. Phibes is after it."

"Then we have two options, Mr. Trout. A standoff, or let's get on with it and let the best man win. Good night, Inspector."

"Good night, Mr. Biderbeck."

The dark man slipped inside the tent flap, his eyes still flashing, still defiant. Trout had to admire him. For all his spiffiness, he'd spun out to close a half a million quid on this jaunt, came near to blowing it, and he was still ready to risk it all on a showdown. If the bastard would only spill out maybe he could help him. Nothing was worse than an academic with his professional secret stuck away in the woodwork. Well, it was too late to change his mind, too late to do a lot of things. That business at Margate got him into the thing in the first place. Maybe it was a sign. Anyway, Phibes would make his move soon enough.

He pulled his hands out of his pockets and started running. The sand bounced up like cotton puffs around the string. The moon was high now and the trucks and the tents had silver patches on them. The flag caught an edge of wind and flapped, making the only other sounds in the camp.

Later the wind came up. It built slowly but steadily. Gusts here and there, sand riffs, then it slowed, caught volume, and came on stronger, scouring the trucks. The flag wrenched at the pole, tent flaps banged, and the camp bent under the air draft. The wind was in good voice now, splintering everything with its pressure, probing the camp with its force.

But the tents stood quite firm on their well-planted stakes, and their occupants were undisturbed behind the canvas.

Hackett droned up his own storm, immobilized beneath

the keg where his friend had providently wrapped him in a handy sack and left him to fight his own demons. Hackett would have survived an earthquake.

Division Chief Waverly slept the sleep of babes, his usually fluorescent face softened to pink by the kind of fulsome slumber that comes to men of his temperament. He had wrestled with the logistics of his assignment throughout the day. He had conceived a plan and had seen to it that it would be carried out. Now he slept, the waves of contentment washing new resolve into his fibers.

His subordinate also slept, not as well, but slept nevertheless. Trout was certain about no thing, less about any man. He knew too well what his chief intended, knew also that Biderbeck could be trusted not to be trusted. Phibes, unless the variables took over, would be calling the shots. The storm howled with conviction. Only his muscles, unlimbering from the run, kept him from waking.

Biderbeck and Diana were awake, or they were awake only to each other. The sandstorm—ten sandstorms—could not have disturbed them.

Rosemont Baker slept, too. He was supposed to stand guard, to be a watchful sentry over the sarcophagus. He had made a promise to Mr. Biderbeck and he knew how important *that* was. But the ale, combined with one last cigar and a book that didn't make sense anyway, combined to bring his chin on his chest, where it rested now.

An awful gust shook the camp, sending a spray of sand over Biderbeck's legs which were snaking out of the cot. He reached over to close the flap, returning very quickly to Diana's seeking mouth.

Baker, possessed of no such pleasures, woke up. Perhaps it was just as well, because he'd fallen asleep on top of his sleeping bag and was now shivering with cold. He threw his boots off and dived back into his bag, zippering it up over his head.

Hackett belched, emitting a groundswell enough to tear the earth, had his mouth been so positioned.

The wind ripped the Union Jack, sending it into a defiance that would have done credit to Nelson at Trafalgar. The flagpole clattered and shook. Gusts of sand scoured and scathed the trucks. A whooping blast, like ten thousand Midianites riding from ambush, swept through the camp's defenses. The trip wire did its fearsome best. Glass shards and empty green bean cans danced the line. The jerrycans shouldered together spelling the holocaust. The flagpole announced great defiance and did not bend. The flag echoed Nelson and the Very pistols awaited their triggers.

The Midianites galloped on, joined by the Medes, Assyrians and the mighty Babylonians. Kings, great warrior kings, drove their hordes to the slaughter, swinging mace and battleaxe in preparation for the victory. Sargon, Assurbanipal, and Nebuchadnezzar shouted orders. Rameses, Solomon and Saul reined their chariots. Belshazzar and Xerxes raised arms. A thousand battle horns sang in reply.

A new dust wall raised fury on the right. It swirled, parted, swirled again in furious clatter. Ten thousand horses cadenced. About them countless scimitars sang. Like diamonds caught on fabled mine walls, steel gleamed. Above, the moon froze it all.

A wall of sound crashed the center. A lowered pause of dust, a crack of speared arms unfurling, and the Hyksos horde spelled a new doom.

The camp slept on, unwarned, unrepentant to its danger. Diana sighed in new latitudes of relief. Waverly dreamt: dreamt of guns, dossiers and legions of decent citizens protected by his long and watchful arms. Trout sulked, a ball of zipper risible in his ribs. The bulbous Hackett, ungirdled and unbelched of multiple volumes of air, snored like a sea of sharks.

Outside the warrior host advanced. Hyksos, Midianite, and Philistine converged. The buckled and cutlassed Assyrian levies led the van. Horses chafed. Swords were pulled and angled to a line. Sargon, all-conquering Sargon, raised his arm and beard in ferocious signal. Baker's tent was engulfed. The wind hung, caught, and erupted into new cataclysms of energy. The host swirled about sleeping Baker's tent, caught up on its defenses, rallied, then brought up a new threat A strange and awesome war engine, its powerful jaws designed to crack the most obstinate enemy, lumbered to the squat tent, its pinions and gears set to their finite motion, and its mechanical summations unleashed against all resistance.

The walls of the tent bent, tore, and opened.

The iron jaws, aligned in inevitability, sheared the canvas.

Baker slept on.

Outside ten thousand kings waited. Ten thousand bows announced their mighty presence. Ten thousand horses marched in cadence. Ten thousand throats raised the cry.

The wind, the awful wind wailed. The battle engine replied.

Baker slept.

Metal jaw rose to meet metal jaw in a straight mechanical line, unyielding, catching cot end to cot end, crushing; closing cloth top to cloth bottom, inclusive; pressing head to feet, Baker, pressing on his incompressible bone to incompressible bone.

The trumpets blazed the charge. The wind winnowed

the scimitar host. Priests threw bones to battle's outcome.

Baker rose, tried to, found his throat, screamed, tried to rise, get his armor, blast, kill the buggers, tried to get up, rose inches, half-inches, not enough, screamed through broken throat, rose in parts to scream again from torn edge of bone to broken bone, could rise no more, reached his last strength of wrist to the gun, would have pulled, felt again blood and broken bits of bone instead. The jaws came on and he, seeing his enemy now, knowingly withheld his later screams, wanting to get up like a man and die with a bit of honor. Just a bit of honor . . .

The winds rolled. The host, that terrible host, rode. The jaws closed.

Jonathan Biderbeck was asleep, his head nestled amongst Diana's still tingling tits, when the wind stopped. Hackett looked enormous, was enormous under the table, his snores loud enough to frighten him from ever awakening. Harry Trout sought other areas in his sleeping bag and his chief heard the judge's gavel and the gallows fall simultaneously loud enough to hear nothing else.

Like Megiddo ending in sweeping triumph, the truck burst out of Baker's surrendered tent and was away before it or any other sounds aroused the camp.

Quickly, very quickly, its twice-precious contents were restored by a vindicated Anton Phibes to their original chamber inside the mountain. The flushed fright that had gathered and almost broken his remnant senses fled with the last grindings of the truck's motors. His hands regained their surgical calm, his chin its previous resolve. All that had been lost was recovered. Victoria was with him now, and ready. Their journey, once begun and so rudely cut short, could continue, and not an instant too quickly. The moonclock was running. It had grown very late indeed.

But he had to see her once yet before their final reunion.

Delaying his evening's exertion for a moment he motioned to Vulnavia to rest the caisson on their route to the royal chamber. He opened the sarcophagus with the proper motion of the snake head to find again the untouched form of his slumbering wife.

"My darling, they have tried to take you from me, and they have failed. I will keep you by my side for these next few hours and then will be revealed to us the true meaning of the conjunction of the Moon, the spirits of Isis, and Osiris and the secrets of Akhenaton's tomb. We shall wait together, we shall find together the River of Life. Together we shall unlock the door to eternal life! Rest, rest, my beloved. Only a few hours more and I shall be at your side."

Reverently, lovingly, he lowered the lid. Hesitantly, surely, he turned the snake head, turned and turned again. And in horror, gross horror most black, he found the key missing! Gone! Severed! Cut from the snake's throat! Gone!!

Biderbeck's camp was routed out of its wrappings the next morning by a shower of whistles and rushing feet. Diana clutched for the anxious skin of her lover and awoke to his harsh absence. Hackett didn't awake; he exploded and groped amidst the table and chair legs and ran to Biderbeck's tent, fearful.

A red Waverly spoke. "Mr. Biderbeck, don't interrupt me. This is the last straw. Shouldn't have listened to you before, against my better judgment. This entire party is leaving, leaving as soon as humanly possible. I *order* you to expedite such movement. It is now 0730. Expect to be away at 0900, very latest. We shall intercept Major Braff and his boys at the Ben Galla oasis if we're lucky and turn this whole hideous business over to the military. Is that understood?"

Trout shot a glare at Biderbeck, was grateful when Hackett stumbled in. As usual, the Chief had spoken so fast that everyone was left without a word. They got up and in that same breathless mood moved out. Baker's death seemed to suspend the whole thing.

He went out in time to see Waverly kick the jerrycans. Hackett was sweeping sand off the truck's windshields. Some of the gear had already been stowed in their vans and one tent was down. The camp was breaking up. He wondered if they'd get away in time.

"Mr. Trout?" Hackett shoved a sack of canned goods into the back of a truck and was calling to him.

"Yes, Hackett, I see you're on top of it."

"Like I should have been last night. If I'd only been up to it I could have gotten the bastard before he put old Baker away. Migod, wasn't that something awful?"

"Dr. Phibes doesn't do things the simple way."

"But he's no bigger'n a crab! Could the man have not defended himself? He had his scatter gun on him."

"Too quick, too dark. Murder's like that. You never know."

"But it takes a crazy mind to do something like that. I should have been there. I might have had a trick or two. It was my watch. That's the hurting part. That's what's so awful. And now we've got to go, before we've finished."

He started to sniffle and slobber. Trout snapped him to.

"Get hold of yourself, man. There's no time for that."

"But I knew old Baker. Knew 'em all, for that matter. And they've gone and we're left with a goose egg."

"It'll be worse than that if we don't get out on schedule. Are you done here, Hackett?"

"Pretty much so, sir." Hackett mopped his face with his sleeve. Trout caught a whiff of his indulgence from the night before, and had to steady himself.

"Then let's get it on. Go in and look after Mr. Biderbeck while I see to this."

"All right, sir. I'll be doing that, sir. On my way, sir. At 0900, right?"

"Right, Hackett."

Trout put his shoulder to the cartons, a two-man job. But he couldn't stand anyone's whimpering, especially not a fat man. It was already a quarter to eight, and a lot could happen before nine.

When Hackett got to the big tent Biderbeck was sitting on his cot. Nothing seemed to have been packed.

"We can strike this tent next, sir. Any time you're ready."

Biderbeck just sat there.

"Sir?"

"Oh . . . in a moment, Hackett. I'll let you know."

Miss Trowbridge brushed past him. Maybe she could take care of things.

"Give you a hand with any of your gear, Miss Trowbridge?"

"No, thank you. I can manage." She didn't seem too interested, either. He'd better leave. Wasn't too welcome in there anyway.

Diana was even less pleased with the situation but she wasn't going to mince words. Baker's death had cut it. And Waverly, for all his bluster, for once had managed some authority.

"Jonathan, you haven't even started to pack."

But that was farthest from his mind. "I can't leave now! I've got the answer right here in my hand, if I can only see it!"

"Oh, Jonathan! Not again! What else has to happen

before you'll give up this ridiculous obsession?"

"Darling, you *think* you know how much this means to me. It means a thousandfold more! I can't turn my back on it now. The *years* I've been on this quest! The fortunes I've spent don't matter. But darling, you've got to believe me, I need only a few hours more." He pulled the gold key from a pouch. "This! And a few hours! Is that asking too much?"

"A few hours for what?"

"I don't know. But deep inside that mountain, at the very moment when the moon is full on the other side of the world and when Sirius, the brightest star in the heavens, meets with Venus ...let me show you where the ancients . . ."

But her patience was gone.

"Jonathan! You don't make sense. You can't know what you're saying. I don't know you any more."

"Don't say that! Help me convince them, please! A few hours!" He looked ragged. "It means my life to me."

She held his heart. She knew it, and she couldn't move even when Waverly came in.

"What's this Hackett tells me, not packed yet, sir? Can't have that, sir. Biderbeck, realize it's a disappointment naturally. Suppose it's like getting a great monster salmon right up to the net and having him break the line, what? But there's more fish in the sea, right? Now I must *insist*, sir. We are moving *out*. Instanter."

And yet they didn't move. Waverly persevered.

"Miss Trowbridge, I say, how about you? You ready?"

She kept watching Biderbeck, then answered finally. "Yes, Mr. Waverly, I am absolutely ready."

"Good, sending you out in the first car. Certain form, after all. Women and children et cetera. Righto, Miss Trowbridge."

Still she watched Biderbeck, who had not moved.

"Definitely, *righto!*"

And then she was leaving—actually leaving Biderbeck. But before they could get through the tent flap they heard a motorcycle drone. They rushed out to see Major Braff, belted and upright, circle the flagpole, salute and stop.

He looked very brave.

And very, very ridiculous.

Chapter 11

Braff held his salute an extra eighth of a second, then revved his bike. The Union Jack, a bit shredded but still sound, floated overhead. The machine was sputtering so hard that the major couldn't have driven it much past Wembley Waverly and his small reception party even if he had wanted to. That curious, urgent military man had his head stuffed into a seedy tam-o'-shanter, his uniform was a cloud of dust and his legs, like the bike, were covered thick with mud. He saluted anyway, for a second time.

"Braff here. Major, Scottish Fusiliers. Mind identifying yourselves, left to right?" He glared at his hosts.

"My name's Biderbeck, Major."

"You're the bloke, eh?" Then he pounced on Trout. "You must be Waverly then."

Waverly didn't like that at all and stepped forward to set things straight. "I'm Chief Inspector Waverly, C.I.D., Scotland Yard. I heard you were coming with a battalion."

But Braff was used to frying bigger fish. "Came on ahead of recco. My men are an hour's march away. Brief you completely soonest." He drew a bead on Trout. "Leaving you as?"

"My man, Trout." Waverly intended to let him see

where the authority hung.

But Braff was already sneering. "Not very military hereabouts, is it? Area needs policing. Well, no matter, why I'm here." He pulled his fob watch out. "Eleven minutes behind schedule. No matter. Most unusual experience. Maps all show permanently dry waddy eleven miles back. Monstrous depression. No reason to doubt military maps, what? Plunged down the bank and found myself up to the hubcaps in water. Absolute flash flood. Queer, eh?"

Biderbeck perked up. "Water?"

"Seemed like the whole bloody mountain sprung a leak."

"Major, say that again." Biderbeck was getting excited.

"Seemed like that whole bloody mountain sprung a leak." Braff soured. "Don't like to repeat myself, Biderbeck, very civilian habit. Not military."

"But what?"

"Sky as blue as Sussex in May. Incredible, whole river of water. Probably seep away by the time you go back. Old Bedouin on a camel at the opposite bank. Very poor English, as a matter of fact, but finally made sense of him, going through all sorts of rigamarole about superstitions and legends. Last time it happened was four hundred, five hundred years ago. Some fanciful myth." He began kicking the mud off his stockings. Then he pulled out a fresh kerchief from his saddlebag and knotting it about his throat, was ready to address the business at hand. "Enough of that. Now, Waverly, you're the ranking individual here. Fill me in on this Phibes bloke. Never been spotted, I understand, but causing all sorts of trouble. Four murders suspected, that right?"

"Five, Major. A grisly one last night." The Division Chief was getting pink again. Braff began to strut, slapping his hands along the edges of his kilt.

"Hm. Bad news. Lax security in camp, eh? Won't happen again. Understand this fellow's probably skulking about that mountain. Bloody big pile. Done it before. Big bang. Couple dozen strikes should do it. Bastard comes out. Good news."

Waverly was pacing with Braff. "Major, I'm delighted you're here and taking charge. I've got the entire camp under control. We're ready to start moving out."

Biderbeck threw the monkey wrench. "Almost, Inspector Waverly..."

Where Waverly would have jumped, the Major sailed through. "One plan, one leader, one set of orders. Right, Biderbeck? Want to be briefed first thing after a wash-up. Don't like to stand around in a filthy uniform. Bad example."

He reversed direction. Waverly had to do a double hop to stay even. "Major, if I may. The moving out of the camp *in toto* will require some planning and logistics. We'll have to be shown where we can expect to meet up with your men."

Braff was getting impatient. He took off his tam and pounded it against his knee. "All mapped out. Good news."

"But I am *very concerned* about Lady Diana, who has also expressed very clearly to me her desire to leave." Waverly, by a series of very rapid tango steps, had maneuvered to where he stood between the Major and the wash area. Braff sized up the Division Chief. For a close minute it looked as if he was going to pop him. Then duty prevailed.

"Good God, man, where is she? Ought to keep women in full sight at all times. No sense of direction out here. Sunstroke. No telling what. Absolutely must send her back with a driver post haste. You have a driver left?"

"Indeed we do. Former Captain Hackett."

"Well, don't stand around, man! Get this Hackett. Bundle the passenger in. Check the fuel, carry extra water, and be off."

But getting Hackett wasn't going to be so easy. Trout was given the assignment while Braff and Waverly repaired to one of the smaller tents to talk strategy. Biderbeck was left to his own dispositions.

Trout checked the tents, calling the rotund Hackett, and found nothing. He even looked into the shambles of Baker's ill-fated retreat. It wasn't a sick smell, but a grey, sweet haze that shivered up from the shredded cloth and wood of the ruined tent. Trout found himself looking at the remains quite closely even though they had been over the grim business earlier. Rust-red flecks of dried blood were sprayed everywhere—on the walls, canvas floor and torn roof. The nightstand and lamp had two ugly strips of red at odd angles. There were no overt signs, and Baker had certainly not cried out enough to be heard, but the place *looked* like he had put up an awful struggle—or some other forces were working.

Hackett wasn't there and he wasn't in the big tent. Biderbeck almost asked Trout to leave when he poked in after the missing fat man. The perimeter was equally vacant although Trout scoured the whole circle. The string was intact. In fact, not a tin can had fallen to the wind. Further, the flagpole still rose with authority and the camp looked surprisingly solid for its ordeal. Too bad they had to leave. Too bad about Biderbeck.

Trout finally found Hackett as he was on his way back to volunteer to take Diana to the Fusiliers personally. He was passing the parked trucks when he heard it: a heavy thrashing and splashing, like someone taking a bath. Someone very big. A walrus or maybe a hippo. A helluva wild sound for the desert at that hour.

He edged closer to the big trucks, then ducked in between two cabs. The hot air splattered him and he felt like a fish fry in between the two metal doors. More splashes and snorts. A steady bathing of big flesh drenching in water. Sputterings and thumbings as if all the animals in a thousand-mile radius had gathered at a waterhole. Trout bent down and peered past the tires. Then he squatted near the axle to get a better look.

There was Hackett not ten feet away, taking his toilet in a water drum. Half-straddling, half-balancing on the drum edge, he would reach a tentative hand into the tepid depths, bring out a fistful of water, and splash the great acreage of his body. He was quite naked, his skin heaving in heavy aqueous globules. His face was twisted; pained, perhaps from his sins of the previous night, but his nudity gave him a sort of youthful purity.

The big man bent forward from the edge, reached for two handfuls of water, slipped and almost slid head first into the drum. Somehow he managed to right himself to plummet dead weight to the ground on the other side. He thudded and bounced twice into the drum, sending a groundswell of water down on his shoulders. When he finally rolled away the mud was clotted concentrically about his belly and into his armpits. Mud slid from his double chins, hung in his ears, and was caked about his heavy flanks. He jumped up and down, but it only oozed lower on his fatness.

Hackett sneezed, shook his head and tried to figure out what to do next. It was hard work. The brain was sunk with its own waterlogging, the muscles were tied in their own fat and fixed with last night's alcohol, and the mouth wasn't right. That was the worst problem: the taste, the head, the mucking sourness, like a flight of beetles dropped right in his kuppers; or a feast of cubebs and chilis, chutney, curry, black pepper sausage, bloodwurst pudding, okra gumbo, fishballs in sour cream, barbecued boar and anise cakes. His throat was fired and burned out. He could put nothing in to cool it, could swallow nothing, could swallow absolutely nothing for fear of stripping his guts. He had to do something.

Hackett moved very testily on the balls of his feet, swaying a little to the dictates of his butterfly gut, until he was directly opposite Trout. If he could get through the washing ritual, he'd be all right. His belly was large, so large that in fact it had a formidable character all by itself. Bulbous grapes of mud hung from its ripples. With his hair matted, the big man looked like a ferocious Etruscan warrior. He stopped moving and gazed heavily at the trucks. Then he turned slowly, very slowly around to address the drum. Something wasn't right. Ah! The drum needed moving. He butted it to the left, then a little bit more, using his belly like a ram. Too much. He sidestepped, butting as he went, slamming, shaping the drum with his belly ram. There! It was done.

Hackett backed off to admire his work. The sweat made a new pattern down his back, and his curly hair was matted from his effort. Then, moving with great ceremony, and glaring to both sides to assure the privacy of the moment, he grasped the edge of the barrel, jackknifed forward and plunged his head into its depths. He was back up again in the same instant, shaking quarts of water from his hair and ears, and moaning a flood of personal hallelujahs. At this revival of life he draped his belly over the edge and plunged in again. This time his feet lifted from the ground, and his posterior fought to retain the center of gravity. It wasn't easy. The sight of the roisterous rump, its twin globes jostling like planets in collision, brought Trout to a slight cough which he wanted to suppress, but the man wouldn't have heard him anyway.

Hackett stayed under longer. When he finally came up the mud was gone and his flabbed skin was the color of lobsters. He whooped, banged the drum with his arm, banged it again, and gargled for life restored. Then he adjusted his girth once more and plunged for the third time. This time he was going to get it all. He splashed his sides and shanks, throwing handfuls of water on his knees and ankles, sprinkling his rump until the caked mud cracked, spread, and finally fled his imprisoned girth. For Trout it was like witnessing the birth of some prehistoric albino dinosaur. For there, under the galling high noon sun above the dead desert surface, was emerging a round, living white plumpness from its shrivelled cocoon. Like all births, this one required many thrashings, groans, and gurglings. Many times Trout thought the whole drum would tumble, sending the exerted Hackett back into the primeval mud, but the mystic laws of generation caught and held the fat man in their immutability. One final flurry of splashes, one ecstatic rippling of skin, and that freshborn rump trotted clear white and glistening into the world.

"Hackett!"

"Huh!" Hackett sober was not Hackett drunk. He certainly wasn't expecting company.

"Here." Trout threw him one of the big orange case wrappings from the back of the truck.

"Oh, it's you, Mr. Trout. You gave me a start. I'm just getting cleaned up before breakfast."

The big man stood there for a minute, shaking water. He looked at the orange cloth in Trout's hand, then back up at Trout.

"What's that?"

Trout smiled. "Your modesty, Hackett. I'm afraid I've interrupted your bath."

Hackett finally got it on. His whiteness began to blush. "Hey, I guess you have!"

He took the cloth and, fashioning a sort of burnoose from its folds, patted his hair down. "First bath in a week. Began to feel like a plot of sand myself. Could feel the bugs coming if I didn't get into some water. Lost my soap so I just dipped instead. The others packed?"

"Almost. Braff is here."

"Braff. Oh, the Scots Major. How's he look?"

"Like he sounds. Came in advance of his men. We've all talked to him already. Wants us up and out by 0900."

"By 0900? That's less than an hour! Why the damn rush?"

"He plans to blow the mountain. Wants us out of here before the fireworks start."

"Must be an artillery man. That's all those chaps know. Boom-boom. What's Biderbeck say?"

"Not much. He's in his tent."

"The damn shame of it. I feel sorry for the man. All set for the big strike, and then some sonuvabitch puts the kibosh on him. Awful damn shame to work that hard for nothing."

"He strikes me as a gambler. He'll come back again. Try something else."

"You don't know Mr. Biderbeck, sir. This was a big one for him. Never really said why. But he had us all built up for it."

"What was your stake, Hackett?"

"Oh, we each had a percentage. But y' know, it was

more'n that. Traipsing around these old ruins you get to see how it was like in the beginning. Sort of living from Day One. Mr. Biderbeck kept it pretty exciting." Hackett shrugged, looked sad. "Why the hell anybody would want to kill for an old grave beats me. You got a book on this Phibes, Inspector. What's your theory?"

"Not much, Hackett, except that he probably wants what Biderbeck wants and neither of them are saying, so we're down to a standoff."

"That's where the Army comes in. I guess we'll never know what's inside that mountain." Hackett grabbed his mud-stiffened clothes.

"Maybe yes, maybe no. And Hackett, the Major wants Miss Trowbridge taken on ahead. Can you take the truck?"

'To where?"

"Some rendezvous point. Ben Galla oasis. Says she'll be safer there."

"No question. I'll grab some stuff in the tent and be right along."

"Don't bother. It's all packed. Water, provisions, maps. You've got one of the rifles, too."

"And you'll bet I'll use it if I can. Even the score on that scurvy bastard."

He swung the orange canvas over his shoulder and whisked off. Trout stared after the bulbous man as he stiff-marched across the sand, a new belligerency girding his loins. Hackett certainly looked as if he meant business.

The leavetaking was efficient and not too unpleasant. Mercifully Waverly and Braff were still closeted in one of the tents. Hackett had found a fresh uniform, his formality fitting the occasion quite well. He hovered over Diana, carrying her travel kit and holding the door for her to get in the car. Then he put the rest of her luggage into the front seat and had a last look at the maps.

She got very busy with her compact while Hackett shuffled his maps. She could see Biderbeck alone and at his desk through the car's rear view mirror. The big tent was otherwise bare of its cartons and equipment. For a long minute their eyes met and held. Then Hackett folded his maps and they were ready.

"May we go?" Diana shut her compact. Hackett put the car in gear, and they were off.

The small field car hummed along the road, molding with its drops and ruts instead of bouncing over them like the trucks. It was rather like sailing; not at all uncomfortable, just boring. The pink sunswept cliffs of Amarna were behind them. The desert spread out all over and went nowhere— and she was going back.

Going back to what?

She hadn't been alone since she was a child. School, dress, social engagements all were selected and passed on by Jonathan. He ran the house, planning the meals down to the vegetable course, scheduling the chores so that she could tell what day it was by whether the mirrors were polished or not, and ruled the servants with a distant autocracy. It was the same way with her acquaintances. Jonathan approved each of her guest lists, weeding out the "negatives," as he called them, with unerring disdain. Travel was equally proscribed. When she was younger, it had been Devon and a week of skiing in Austria. For her sixteenth birthday Jonathan had given her a cruise to Delphos, and a similar cruise each summer after that.

Indeed, Jonathan Biderbeck took care of *everything*. It was hard to leave him, even worse to wonder when he would come back. Or *would* he come back?

The car went on, the sand went on, and her thoughts

went on to her lover. She looked out, then down at her hands, clasping and unclasping. There was nowhere else to look.

The car went on. The sun went on. It was hot. The tears stopped. She looked out. There was something.

"I say, look over there on that dune." She tapped Hackett's shoulder.

"It is *something!* Men marching on the horizon." Music rose. High, reedy music. She recognized it. "A Highland Laddie." The Fusiliers!

But they were going in the wrong direction. Not toward the camp, but away. Were they lost?

Hackett stopped the car. "Highland Laddie" could have led a division, an army. The men marched sharply, knees straight and high, tarns angled to the sun.

The bagpipes tore the air open. Diana thought of the others at the camp. "They're headed the wrong way!"

Hackett was out of the car. "Hey! Fusiliers! Over here!!"

He waved his arms. They kept marching, getting further and further away.

"I'm sorry, miss. I'm going to have to stop them."

"Of course. Hurry."

Hackett rummaged around the front seat for his hat but couldn't find it. He started to fizzle, sweat patched his shirt and his breath whistled out of his fat lips. Then he found something, a *kefillah*. He wrapped the bright mustard-colored cloth around his head and ran after the Fusiliers, who were just disappearing over a dune. The sand was up to his ankles but he ran as fast as he could. Had to get those blokes turned about before they wandered off and got lost. Probably raw recruits first time away from Glasgow.

He shoved his way to the top of the dune and charged down. They were still too far away to shout them down.

Diana watched him bounce over the rim. Then she was alone, except for the very distant bagpipes and the percolating heat. She began to fan herself.

Hackett was running in slow motion. His legs were like sausages, cooking on a griddle. His khakis were drenched. The *kefillah* dripped from sweat. But they were just up ahead, a few more steps.

"Hey!"

Goddammit! A bunch of dummies! Wooden dummies dressed in kilts. The needle on the hidden Victrola started to scratch, then stopped. "Highland Laddie" stopped. The dummies stopped.

Hackett roared. Somebody was playing with him! He kicked into the dummies, smashing heads and arms and legs into the sand, crushing the wood on the dune. He was savage, a tower of furious strength, a gross avenger on a lonely dune. He swung and kicked until his hands and legs trembled with rage. Then he stopped. An awful thought came.

Miss Diana was alone! He'd left her alone!

Hackett ran. Bursting with fury and fear he ran down into the depression and up the other side. He saw the car and another car pulling away—a low black car kicking dust, travelling fast.

The bastards! Hackett was roaring again, and running, running as fast as he could.

But they had taken her. He jumped into the front seat. He could still see the long car up ahead. He stuck the key in and grabbed his rifle. He'd catch the bastards!

He turned the key. Heard a new sound. Looked. Looked right into the absolute last thing he'd ever see.

The fuel gauge popped. The sand jet behind it blew out both of his eyes. His face died in a glut of blood and bone.

He didn't know what had hit him. He panicked, froze, and took the full force of the sandblast. His memory was red.

The gearshift kicked into reverse. The car moved backward, his foot heavy on the pedal. The sand tore his bone; his memory died. He died. The car filled with sand and kept moving.

Minutes later it jolted into the camp and crashed into the water drums, dragging them with it to the palm tree where it finally rammed to a stop, the motor running.

Biderbeck was out of his tent running to the car. "Diana! Diana!" His voice was a moan.

Trout had just finished loading one truck. He saw the damned thing rush by looking like a grey Juggernaut. Sand was still sputtering from the dashboard. By the time he got to the palm tree it had stopped. The car was filled with sand up to the top of the seats. What was left of Hackett—a polished skull and his skeletal arms—stuck in the sand up front. He reached past the bones and turned off the ignition.

Biderbeck had the back door open and was digging fast and quietly. His face was set, as if he was willing away any new wrong turn of luck. He hardly noticed Hackett, hardly noticed anything. He just kept scraping the sand out of the truck.

Trout stepped away. There was nothing, absolutely nothing he could do. The pile of sand outside the car was pretty deep by the time Braff and Waverly came up. They waited to poke around but Trout held them off. Finally Biderbeck finished. Only Hackett was in the car. Waverly was the first to say anything.

"Any sign of her?"

"No, she's . . . she's vanished." Biderbeck had only had a reprieve! He was now thinking of other possibilities.

So was Braff. "I can see I am going to need an alternate plan. He must be a fiend. Trout, take care of the remains. Probably comes under a special situation section, military burial, right?" He shifted to Biderbeck and scowled.

"Mr. Biderbeck! I'll want you at the briefing, sir!"

Waverly, who had arrived on the scene speechless, left in the same condition, his arm bent to Braff's. The Major's control was now quite complete. He had put on a fresh set of kilts over equally freshly laundered khakis. To round out the image, he had dusted his tam-o'-shanter to a shine and stuck a sprig of palm leaves into its puff. Twin cartridge belts fortified his chest, a dirk was thrust in his belt, and another gleamed evilly from his right argyle. On his right side he wore the heaviest Army service revolver Trout had ever seen. It was a regulation .38-caliber but fitted out with a carved elephant tusk handle larger than a man's fist. In close quarters a smack from that knob could be as lethal as a bullet from the other end. To complete his violent visage, Braff had wrapped his waist with a leopard skin cummerbund which pulled his form into weight-lifter proportions and implanted an audible portent to his breathing. Braff both looked and sounded intimidating.

The voluptuous black cheroot stuck in his mouth made him smell that way, too.

On their way to the conference the Division Chief recovered his senses, and with them some of his pride.

"Braff!"

"*Major* Braff, sir. Lose rank and you lose control. Lose control and you've lost the situation." Braff speeded up his step.

"In any case, and *irregardless,* sir, it's 0945. Your advance men have not yet arrived. Not only are *they* late, but we have lost one member of this expedition and another member is missing—both casualties occurring during the execution of an order issued by you, sir!"

Braff pulled up and faced the Division Chief. "The order was issued to correct a situation, a deteriorated situation brought on by the lack of leadership, theretofore!"

"Sir?!"

"I said, lack of leadership *theretofore!* Who led this expedition, Mr. Waverly?"

Waverly reddened, always a difficult sign. "It is a private venture, organized, paid for and led by British subjects."

"Who led this expedition? Sir!"

"... 'to advance the causes of antiquarian knowledge.' I quote from a license issued by the Foreign Ministry to Mr. Jonathan Biderbeck. A copy is on file at our Embassy in Cairo."

"You make me repeat myself, sir. WHO LED THIS EXPEDITION? Who was the responsible public official in charge during the initial phases of its difficulties?" Braff's voice lowered to a growl. His tam shook increasingly.

Waverly's pinkening grew worse. He watched the other man for a respectable time, then did what he did best: exploded.

"It was *I* who was asked by the Home Office to come out to Egypt. It was *I* who first spotted the criminal pattern in the whole 'affaire Biderbeck." It was *I* who linked that pattern with a known public enemy. And it was *I* who turned the whole Phibes case open in the first place. *No one in the Department* knows as much about Anton Phibes as *I* do—except Trout, of course."

"Except how to catch him."

"That was uncalled for. You are overstepping your authority, Braff." Waverly was up on the balls of his feet, glaring right at the kilted military man. But Braff stood his ground.

"I said what I said and I meant it. Oh, I heard about you chaps, all right. Hopping around London with your magnifying glasses into the sidewalks while them medicos got rubbed out wholesale. And the bucko crawled through your whole lineup before you had a chance to sneeze. You were in charge then, too, weren't you, Inspector Waverly?"

"Don't press me, sir, or I shall have to see your credentials!"

"See my credentials? This is my credential." Braff pointed to his gun belt.

"Then where are your troops? They're overdue. Miss Trowbridge is missing—and a murderer is roaming around those hills planning the next outrage. I repeat, Braff, where are your men?!"

"They will arrive *as ordered*. Part of their training is to follow rules." Now it was Braff's turn to intimidate the smaller Division Chief. He started stalking around the flagpole, Waverly backtracking. "And then we will deal with your Doctor Phibes, Inspector. In a military fashion. Clean. Quick. Decisive. No quarter asked and none given."

A special evil grin framed Waverly's face. "How? Dynamite? You don't even know if he's still up there. Aeroplanes? You could shoot up the whole desert. Or maybe you're planning to sabotage him?"

"Something like that."

"*Something like that!* You mean you don't know?"

Braff started to ramble. "One battalion isn't enough. The fiend has accomplices. Probably a whole network of 'em. Working with the locals. After the gold, or oil—that's it, the oil! They're in the employ of a foreign power. Lot of hostility toward the Empire, you know. Saw it myself. I was with

Kitchener, you know. They don't like us in these parts. Treachery, intrigue. All happened during the war. Before then it was all peaches and cream. Couldn't get enough of British customs. Rugby, polo, bowling. Played all over the world today. But the war changed it all. Too much jealousy. Then we beat the pants off the buggers and now it's worse. Phibes *is* an Austrian by birth, isn't he? Probably working with those sneaky Hapsburgs. They never did understand fair play on the continent."

They were circling the flagpole at a hop. Both men were sweating from their verbal battle, but being gentlemen and men of honor neither was ready to concede anything to his rival. It was a question of professional competency. The sun, of course, goaded their efforts, and nobility struggled for survival in that sparse desert outpost.

That virtue was still in good preservation thirty minutes later when Trout, somewhat the worse for his exertions with Hackett's last rites, approached his Chief for further instructions. The hour of departure had come and gone. All the tents except the large one had been stricken, the trucks partly loaded, and water and food stores stocked at the ready. The expedition was ready to expedite if someone would give the signal.

"Sir," Trout was obliged to speak only after he had watched the tandem leadership stalk each other for a full minute without a word passing.

"Keep out of this, Trout!" Braff growled.

"He's my man. He'll keep out on *my* orders. Trout, you hear me?" Waverly stood on his honor.

"Yes, sir. Reporting that the camp is ready to be stricken, sir. Came to take the colors."

"Take the colors! But my men are en route. Got to be able to see us if they're going to get here. What time is it?"

"Ten hundred hours, sir."

"Good Lord, they must be late. Not like them. The young officers, their fault. No sense of direction or duty. Mr. Waverly, I suggest we get out of this ruddy sun and repair to that tent over there where we can work up a plan that works, and get it working."

"You can expect our cooperation, me and my man Trout here. Our department always works with the military. Helped you catch the spies during the war." The Division Chief, being the big man about it all, crossed over to the Major and led him off the field. Honor thus preserved, they were ready for the exigencies of the day. And Waverly, as he usually did when he felt that he was coming into the upper hand, turned affable. "Now you'll help us. We're all in the same war anyway; good against bad, law against evil and all that. Trout!"

Trout was pulling at the colors.

"Trout!"

"Salute before you do that!"

Braff beamed. "Good thinking, Inspector."

The three men, sweated and dusty as they were, ramrodded to attention and each gave as smart a salute as you could find, thus preserving patriotism as well as honor in the lonely outpost. Then the two mollified leaders proceeded to their command center with the Division Chief issuing one last instruction before they left the field.

"Trout, locate Mr. Biderbeck and have him join us forthwith. Time to move ahead."

Trout snapped to. Biderbeck was still staring at the sand-filled truck so Trout just transmitted the executive order and returned to the loading.

Biderbeck nodded, said nothing. When Trout was gone he got up and started to poke around the car. He sifted the sand, digging deeper in hope of finding something, anything that would give some hint of Diana's whereabouts.

Then, deep under the sand in the front seat, he found it: a miniature sarcophagus complete in every detail to the larger one he had taken from the mountain.

He rubbed it clean and pressed the snake head. The lid opened.

Inside was a piece of white paper, folded into a tiny quarto.

He opened it carefully. His fingers tensed. "*Come Alone!*" flowed across its surface in a thin, elegant script.

"Biderbeck! Are you coming?" Braff shouted from the command post.

But they could go to hell. They all could go to hell.

Biderbeck put the note in his pocket. Then he dug his hand deeper into his jacket. The snake head key was there.

"Righto, Major."

Biderbeck slipped out past the tent flap, then walked along the back of the tent and away from the camp.

He was going to the mountain.

Chapter 12

It was a long, dry, dead route to the mountain. A long, slow, dead route to the mountain. A tired weary way, travelled thousands of years, thousands of years ago; a heavy, mournful way; an immemorial way.

The small truck moved down the valley floor. The mile of violet-grey walls buffered its engine, absorbed its penetration. Its tires used up the dust dodging rock litter. It rode at its own pace.

The air was quiet under the baking sun. The hot air caught the light, fixed the light. Perfect to the millennia tangent, the sun fixed the air and made the light a line. The sun disk rode the sky.

The dry air caked his throat and stung his skin. The rocks slammed against the fender, bounced to the frame and broke. Dead rocks bounced and broke. The dust rose from behind his truck. He wanted to think of it all but the sun was hot. The sun was high and the men were dead and the time had come.

And Diana.

The air was a wordless echo against the rock, straining and calling upon itself, trying to remember a parallel time, a parallel place. The tires ran, the sun was up high and he thought of her, gone. Diana.

When time spent, the sun went, light was gone and the hour fled. He'd be dead. Yes, he'd be dead.

And the clock within the mountain tolled it all: registered the characteristic names, the memorial place and the accumulation of all time there, among the mountains of that place.

He rushed and stopped the retroactive wonderment. He calculated the dice and the throws of discontent. He figured on knife edge after knife edge the balance sheets of *that* specific he was going to do.

And he stopped in the dust and rock and got out under the sharp sun and heavy blue sky; the heaviest sharp blue sky. And he got out of the car. And walked through the dust. And went into the mountain.

The cave was black and bare. He went to it and stood. Glanced at the sky and sun and felt the agnostic heat of a valley of dead gods. Listened for the crucial calamitous sounds of their memorials. Listened for the whisper of the mourners' feet, and the intransigent prayer of the severed sigh above. He listened. And heard nothing.

Biderbeck went into the cave. He put his light on. He felt the gravel dust boot in the angle of his pace, felt the invitation of the space beyond, saw the accumulations of all that he had observed before, walked, passed, plunged past black open space, his light proving.

He walked further, deeper into that illumined blackness. He thought only of what he could lose; thought only of what he could lose. And Diana.

He probed on through the darkness, through the black hole darkness. Past the symbols and bits of bone, past all swords and shields, past the last touch of what it was to blackness; to blackness and the probe of his white, stiff light.

Then the music came.

Silence. Stones to walking feet. A pertinent breath to the probed light. Silence.

Then the music came again.

Came, swelled, rose, billowed. Rose again in constant volume increments. Rose to rock bounding against rock, a calamitous echo of sounds. Organ sounds. Sweet, metal-throated organ sounds.

He ran. He started running. And ran. Fast.

His footsteps filled the cave. Bounced. Echoed back.

He kept running through the black rocks and into the blackness. The music ran at him, echoed, bounced and stopped. The music stopped.

He ran against the silence. But the music had stopped. The cave was silent. The music had stopped. And she was missing.

Then he saw a light. With the music gone, Diana gone, everything gone, he saw a light and ran toward it.

He raced down the tunnel where the music had stopped. Raced down the dark tunnel and into the light. Raced into the light and into the room where the organ was. And saw the organ, the light and a girl.

And Phibes!

The man wasn't like what he had thought. He was a strong, gentle, well-contained man. A comely man. A man of intent and parts. A man who had a reason to be there. He spoke.

"So, Mr. Biderbeck. At long last we meet face to face. I am glad you have the knowledge to find me. And the courage to come."

His first thought was her. "Where is Diana?"

"You may see her in a moment. In fact, you may yourself unlock her door with the key I know you have!"

So that was it. He took out the gold snake's tongue. Phibes went on.

"Of course, a lucky find for you, Biderbeck. A twist of fate for me. Give it to me and Diana will be returned to you."

"You think me a fool, Phibes? You underestimate me! I too have studied the archaeological history of this mountain, its legends, and records known to few other men! I have studied them longer than you yourself! Don't you think I know what this can unlock?"

"No! Only *I* know! You are close to the secret. But only *I*, standing in this room, have deciphered the last secret of all! Give it to me, Biderbeck! It's of no use to you otherwise!"

Phibes' voice grated in anger. "Every minute that you wait you will regret!"

But Biderbeck pressed. "Don't you think I know the unique position of this mountain? The great forces in the heavens which are coming into conjunction above this very spot even as we talk?"

"Then you know there is no time to lose! Do you love Diana?"

"Why do you want this key? What does it mean to you?"

Phibes grew enraged, his voice cracking like glass. "I ask you one more time. Do you love Diana?"

Biderbeck hesitated. Phibes probed.

"Do you love her?"

"And I ask you—why do you need this key?"

"For my beloved wife! For Victoria for whom I have killed and would gladly kill again, as well you know!"

"Your wife is dead?"

"And once was I! But I live now. And so shall she!" Phibes glared at Biderbeck and went on. "Give it to me,

Biderbeck, and you shall have your Diana! If not, I cannot answer for her. Or for you."

Biderbeck looked at the key, his voice almost a whisper. "She can never know what she means to me. And no one can ever know what *this* means to me!"

Rebuffed, Phibes was approaching the end of his patience. "It is only because I respect the knowledge which you possess, and acknowledge that in other circumstances you and I could learn much from each other, that I offer you one more chance. Now — will you give me that key?"

Phibes' hand rose to the Wall, gears slid on metal chutes. The filigree screen behind the man opened. And she was there.

His heart ran into the side of his chest. His parched throat wanted to cry, and cried. Cried deep, inverted to catch the rise of his breath. Pulse and eyes unquiet, far-seeing, bent toward her, hands slowly rising, caught in glass. The angles sharp and bright. Awfully bright angles, and chutes. And passages. A dazzling edge of angles removing her, catching him. Parting them again.

He was there with her but he had to get her from inside the glass pyramid. That much he recognized. Phibes spoke.

"She can hear you," (he didn't remember speaking), "but for reasons you shall soon learn she is temporarily unable to utter a sound."

His legs pressed. He wanted to go. She was there, the cylinder deep around her. Not right. His legs pressed. The flashlight. He'd smash the pyramid with the flashlight.

"Wait, Biderbeck!"

The glass mirrors grew grey from smoke. Smoking grill. Hot smoking oily grill. Hot smoke poured with oozing oil. The oil spread down, seeping hot, and rose against the outer walls. The space was small between where he was and a larger cylinder. All through the glass he saw the oil, hot and smoking, rise. Phibes again was goading.

"In exactly six minutes the boiling oil will rise to the top. And flow into your Diana's prison."

He wanted to smash Phibes. No time. No time for that. He would have gotten to him but there was no time for that. The hot oil smoke seeped on live rings. It pressed hot, higher.

"It is out of my hands completely. The decision is now yours, Biderbeck. If in six minutes you can traverse the maze, using your wisdom and your ingenuity, and if you unlock the last door, *using that key,* she will be safe! But the key will be mine! Choose, Biderbeck! *The key or Diana!*"

That was it, then—the millennial payoff. One late registration of Akhenaton's wish, unfated against the heavens. An atrocious gamble begun in heresy and carried in silence. Beating scavengers and the constant pressure of marauders to split into parallel evocations, Phibes' and his own. Brought down now to the final hour in five million, still racing the clock.

Automatically he moved in. He was going to win his bet.

The entrance was easy enough. The maze of passageways were tall enough to walk upright. Keeping Diana in front of him he walked straight up to the ramp, was ready to go on, and bumped into a glass wall. Phibes goaded him.

"Not *too* fast. The clues are all around you. And you still have five minutes. While you're working, Biderbeck, note how the level of the oil is rising." The smoke and heat was higher now. He veered off, read some Arabic to find the true entrance panel. It moved easily and- he was in.

Then it got harder. The glass walls narrowed into a

parallelogram. He crawled, inching forward in slow progress. He could hear the oil now, hissing. A small opaque glass was up ahead. He pressed it.

A coil of awful hissing scalded the glass chute. Snakes! A boiling clot of snakes. His reflexing hand grabbed the panel and pulled it shut. The snakes struck the glass just as he got his fingers away.

He smelled the oil. He walked slower now, calculating his approach. No time for accidents. No time for mistakes. No time for anything but the precise move.

A figure, in glass, was up ahead. Very stiff, very warlike. He broke off the spear tip and, scoring the glass walls, moved on.

The glass shimmered now. The oil's head floated in the passageway. It smelled stronger.

Again the corridor narrowed. He edged sideways, feeling the head closer. The glass passed smooth, then indented. Some sort of shelf. Inside was a huge tarantula, all legs and beak, crawling.

He slid down and eased himself along. The walls were still narrow but he could get away from it Wait! A mirror! He was moving toward the tarantula!

It was crawling behind him now. It moved off the shelf and dropped down.

He looked over his shoulder. The tarantula was on the floor, and coming!

He inched ahead through the narrow glass, squeezing into a wider space. He ran the few paces to a low door. The tarantula was moving, coming fast. The door was shut hard!

He smelled the oil. Could feel the hard heat now. But the tarantula was coming.

He pulled. Twisted. Pulled. And was through into a large corridor. He slammed the door back and the thing was crushed bloody across the floor, its legs striking the air.

Diana was a few feet away. The only way to her lay through a narrow tunnel between the larger and small cylinder. A few inches remained before the oil would hit the top. He could hear the sizzling and the air was stiff with heat as he bent to crawl through.

He lunged on his hands and knees in heat intense enough to strip the skin. Lunged through the pain that was the air. Crawled on skin seared by the glass to the shrill persistent pressure of the oil. Crawled through the cooking air along the glass wet with his own pain. Crawled where he could barely see or breathe, crawled under the pall of smoke and haze, crawled into a living streak of pain, crawled until his thoughts and time ran out.

His hand contained enough sensation for him to feel the key within it. Enough to place it in the last door remaining between him and Diana.

The door opened and rose upward. Phibes' voice intoned, "My congratulations, Mr. Biderbeck. And my eternal thanks."

The key passed to Phibes' hands. While Biderbeck struggled to free Diana, Phibes swept off and, leading his elegantly clad assistant, descended a small flight of stone stairs at the edge of the room. Biderbeck watched as the strange, courtly couple crossed a shallow water channel to reach the golden doors beyond. The doors of the Osiris papyrus, the same doors planned by Akhenaton's builders to come in view once every half-millennium! The key that he had given over to Phibes fit their sculptured lock and Phibes passed through.

But *he* had Diana.

"Darling ....are you all right?"

She clutched him. He half-led, half-carried her until

they were out of the pyramid and away from the oil. Then she finally spoke.

"Now I am. Are you?"

The large doors were closing. Phibes and the girl moved off on the water beyond. Their barge, elegant and carved as any royal replica, contained the flower-draped bier of his wife.

Phibes saluted his opponent. "Farewell. In some other time, some other world, we may meet again!"

The doors closed. The golden doors of immortality closed. The moonclock stopped.

But not the oil. It was above the cylinder edge and spilling.

Biderbeck grabbed Diana and led her up another small staircase to an antechamber just as a racing jumble of approaching steps announced their protectors.

"Who's there? Are you all right? Where's Phibes? Thank God you're safe!"

Braff burst in, hatless in his haste. The two policemen were right behind.

"We heard him, didn't we?"

"I'm afraid you are too late, gentlemen. He was here. But his boat sailed."

"What bloody nonsense is that, Biderbeck? A boat inside a mountain." Braff's jaw jutted.

"A royal barge. Sailing on the Egyptian equivalent of the River Styx. The River of Life, of Immortality. And in a few moments Doctor Phibes will know all the secrets which lie at its end."

"Then I'll bring a gun boat upriver. Man has to come out some place, what? Well, no use wasting time here. Long as you're both fit. Reports to file, wireless to send to H.Q. Come along men, step lively. Lady Diana, can you make it on your own?"

Diana had recovered. "Of course, Major, thank you."

Braff led them all back the way they had come. Biderbeck lingered, looking at the ancient room with an equally ancient nostalgia. Diana ran to him, gathered him in her arms.

"Thank God *you're* safe. And *I'm* safe. And this nightmare is over!"

She shook and wept tears of joy; her hair was perfume in his face.

Then something else had him, was taking him, was pressing and pushing his features— something that had pushed him every hour of every day for the last memorable thousands. Pushing him hard and close now. Pushing him with timeclock momentum, running on, running on.

But he had nothing to stop it now. The vial was empty. The doors had closed.

The timeclock had run out.

Diana pulled back, brushed his skin again with her hair to kiss him. And she saw him.

The timeclock ran out, and she saw him.

She had only wanted to kiss him, but she saw him when the timeclock ran out.

He begged her understanding with his eyes.

And died.

Dr. Phibes Rises Again!
Copyright © 1971 William Goldstein
ALL RIGHTS RESERVED

**Visit + "Like" + "Share"
"DR. PHIBES"
on facebook:**
http://www.facebook.com/pages/Dr-Phibes/189893094376380

Stay tuned - more Dr. Phibes coming soon!
Dr. Phibes The Real Androbots©

Featuring more of
'Sophie'

The newest of the wondrous
Clockwork Wizards©

Dr. Phibes The Real Androbots©
Copyright © 2013 William I. Goldstein and
Damon J.A. Goldstein
ALL RIGHTS RESERVED
WILLIAM I. GOLDSTEIN
DAMON J. A. GOLDSTEIN
T 3 1 0. 3 8 4. 7 8 1 6
E forever@earthlink.net

Like" + "Share"

"THE CULT-CLASSIC DR. PHIBES SERIES"

on Facebook:

https://www.facebook.com/DrPhibesVulnaviasSecret
https://www.facebook.com/DrPhibesInTheBeginning
https://www.facebook.com/DrPhibesRisesAgain
http://www.facebook.com/pages/Dr-Phibes/189893094376380

Visit our blog:

http://authorized-dr-phibes-blog.blogspot.com/

The AUTHORIZED DR. PHIBES BLOG by the author of
'THE CULT-CLASSIC DR. PHIBES SERIES'

Visit and watch our Youtube Channel:

FOREVER PHIBES VIDEO CHANNEL

http://www.youtube.com/user/FOREVERPHIBES

"THE CULT-CLASSIC DR. PHIBES SERIES"
Visit + "Like" + "Share"
"Dr. Phibes" on Facebook today and
become a Dr. Phibes Phan Forever.

http://authorized-dr-phibes-blog.blogspot.com/
https://www.facebook.com/DrPhibesVulnaviasSecret
https://www.facebook.com/DrPhibesInTheBeginning
https://www.facebook.com/DrPhibesRisesAgain
http://www.facebook.com/pages/Dr-Phibes/189893094376380

– ATTENTION ALL DR. PHIBES PHANS –

ORIGINAL DR. PHIBES SERIES BOOK COVERS

THE CULT-CLASSIC *DR. PHIBES SERIES*

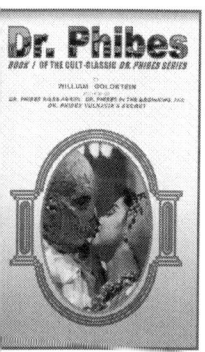   

NEW DR. PHIBES SERIES
COLLECTORS BOX-SET SPECIAL EDITION BOOK COVERS

NOW *EXCLUSIVELY* AVAILABLE
- ONLY THROUGH OUR -
AUTHORIZED DR. PHIBES BLOG:

http://authorized-dr-phibes-blog.blogspot.com/

Buy and read all four today and become a Dr. Phibes Phan
Forever!

THE CULT-CLASSIC *DR. PHIBES SERIES*

WILLIAM I. GOLDSTEIN is the creator of **DR. PHIBES** and the best selling author of **THE CULT-CLASSIC DR. PHIBES SERIES** including **DR. PHIBES, DR. PHIBES RISES AGAIN!, DR. PHIBES IN THE BEGINNING,** and the just recently published **DR. PHIBES VULNAVIA'S SECRET.** He is also co-writer of the top grossing horror motion picture **THE ABOMINABLE DR. PHIBES**, starring Vincent Price. The classic horror film has just been re-released in the United States on Blu-Ray as part of The Vincent Price Collection. William Goldstein lives in Los Angeles and is currently busy collaborating with his son **Damon J. A. Goldstein** on **BOOK IV of THE CULT-CLASSIC DR. PHIBES SERIES; DR. PHIBES THE REAL ANDROBOTS.**

For more information about
Dr. Phibes and The Cult-Classic Dr. Phibes Series
contact
foreverphibes@earthlink.net

Half-man, half-monster, Anton Phibes returns for another orgy of bloodletting, this time seeking the Key to Eternal Life. Those who stand in his way must die.

The first victim is removed by a jeweled serpent, which pierces his brain. The second is torn to bits by a ferocious hawk. The third is eaten to the bone by a swarm of scorpions.

Only one man remains—Jonathan Biderback, a mysterious scientist, equally determined to find Eternal Life. But first he must meet Phibes!

In a subterranean cave deep within the Mountains of the Dead, Phibes awaits his last enemy, a grin of triumph twisting his satanic mouth...

JAMES H. NICHOLSON and SAMUEL Z. ARKOFF PRESENT

Dr. Phibes Rises Again!

Starring
VINCENT PRICE
ROBERT QUARRY

Guest Stars:
PETER CUSHING
BERYL REID
TERRY-THOMAS
ORIGINAL MUSIC COMPOSED BY JOHN GALE
WRITTEN BY ROBERT FUEST and ROBERT BLEES
BASED ON CHARACTERS CREATED
BY JAMES WHITON and WILLIAM GOLDSTEIN
DIRECTED BY ROBERT FUEST
EXECUTIVE PRODUCERS:
SAMUEL Z. ARKOFF and JAMES H. NICHOLSON
PRODUCED BY LOUIS M. HEYWARD
AN AMERICAN INTERNATIONAL PICTURE
COLOR BY MOVIELAB

Printed in U.S.A.

ORIGINAL "DR. PHIBES RISES AGAIN!" BOOK II MOVIE TIE-IN BACK COVER
PUBLISHED BY AWARD BOOKS 1971

Made in the USA
Columbia, SC
30 December 2024